BERNARD BECKETT was born in Featherston. His hobbies include daydreaming and borrowing cats. *Jolt* is his third novel. He thinks it's better than the other two.

Or maybe not. Let him know.

Publisher's note: Bernard Beckett's acclaimed first novel *Lester* was published in 1999. His second novel *Red Cliff* was featured in the List of Notable New Zealand Young Adult Books of 2000.

JOLT

bernard beckett

Longacre Press

Published with the assistance of

ISBN 1 877135 50 X

First published by Longacre Press 2001
9 Dowling Street, Dunedin, New Zealand

Reprinted 2002

Cover image by Imagesource
Book & cover design by Christine Buess
Printed by McPherson's Printing Group, Australia

1.

April 15

Once, when I was seven years old, I stole the teacher's chalk. I needed it, for a game I was playing. A girl in my class, her name was Susanna, told on me, and I was kept in all lunchtime. That afternoon I wagged school for the very first time. I looked up Susanna's address in a phone box, walked twenty minutes to her house, and having checked there was nobody home, strangled both her pet rabbits. I can't tell you how much better that made me feel.

I was sent to see a child psychologist who, according to my parents, diagnosed an overdeveloped revenge instinct. I remember there was a lot of talking, and I was made to draw pictures. At some stage he pronounced me cured. He was wrong.

Last night I saw the Doctor and immediately knew what I have to do. I have no choice. I will kill him. I only caught a glimpse of him, across the ward, acting like any doctor acts, as if the cracks the earthquake opened up are deep enough to swallow his past. I wish I could have kept staring, so he might have turned and caught my eye and seen the murder there. Then he might have felt some of the fear that is owed to him. But this is his territory and I am not stupid. Surprise is the only weapon I have.

I understand this and so I survive.

Twelve days ago, if you'd asked me, I wouldn't have been able to say what surviving was, not really. I know it has been twelve days because I heard the newsreader say it, on Lewis's little plastic radio. He has the bed across from me, although he is almost never in it. He is a wanderer, padding up and down the ward all day, his bare feet quiet on the sticky floor. Cleaning comes last, in times like these. His radio is always with him, pressed close to his ear while his free hand fumbles with the opening of his hospital pyjamas, as if he is showing the world how little he has left. Or perhaps he is just pretending, the same way I am. Perhaps he has his own reasons.

Twelve days since the earthquake. The looting is finally under control, if the radio is telling the truth. The road north has reopened, but only to official traffic, and they're saying the airport might never be rebuilt. So people couldn't visit me, even if anyone knew I was here. The power is still out, apart from emergency generators. The official death toll stands at seven hundred and twenty three....

Then Lewis's instincts took him out into the corridor, beyond hearing range, leaving me alone with my thoughts.

Twelve days. There were definitely five days in the bush, I remember that much. And this is the second day in here, since I stopped taking the pills they bring around on the silver trolley with its spastic wheel. So five days are missing. Days spent lying out in the paddock, before I was found, or out cold in here, with lines of forgetting feeding my wrist. Plenty of time for the Doctor to make his plans, to invent excuses for the drugs he thinks he is

giving me. Well I have plans of my own now, plans I will not let
him see. Plans of rabbits, plans of revenge. Plans to take surviv-
ing, and turn it into living again.

2.

I wasn't even going to do PE. Mum wasn't keen. Seventh
form is a time for more academic pursuits, she said, although I knew she was more worried about the cost. Not
that we had any way back then of knowing what the real
cost would be.

Mr Camden sold me on it, the same way he's been doing
for the last fifteen years. There was an options day at the
end of the sixth form, when Heads of Departments talked
to us about our seventh form choices. Most of them shuffled out and mumbled apologetically into overheads you
could tell they didn't much believe in, 'careers in mathemat-
ics', that sort of thing. So it was easy for Mr Camden to
make an impression.

He strode out in front of us and smiled, like we were his
reason for drawing breath. I saw a couple of the teachers
behind him roll their eyes but he didn't notice, or if he did

he didn't care. Mr Camden is a tall man who wears shorts all year round, as if this is proving some point. Simple, practical shorts, he's not the sort who looks for complications. I'd say he'd be fifty. It's the sort of fifty I hope to reach some day, with a face full of interesting lines and eyes that can still hold an audience. Eyes that shone brighter with each component of the course he introduced. Kayaking, Civil Defence, First Aid, Aquatics. Calculus was never going to stand much of a chance.

He built his presentation steadily towards a climax, the annual Coast to Coast expedition which all PE students would be expected to complete. By that stage his arms were waving about as if he was preparing for take-off and his excited words were wrapped in spit. It was the sort of performance that would either hook you instantly or look ridiculous. He caught me in just the right mood.

I was sixteen then and I was bored. It felt like the years were just washing over me. I needed something different. I was ready for Mr Camden and his demented enthusiasm. I signed up on the spot.

3.

April 16

_____ *This is my writing place. I stumbled across it yesterday. It was a risk, taking to walking, but I knew I couldn't stay in that bed any longer, feeling myself wasting away, waiting for him to return. My whole body ached as soon as I moved. I must have been badly hurt, even more than I realised. If I bend too far forward my back is paralysed with pain, my ribs cut at me when I breathe in, and much of my body is yellow with dying bruises.*

From my bed I have a view of the corridor and I have been able to watch the other patients shuffling by. There are many ways of looking crazy and I have developed my own. I walk stooped, as much as my back allows, small steps with my feet barely letting go of the floor, and my mouth hanging open so I can feel the dribble puddling behind my bottom lip. It is the eyes that are hardest, that are most likely to give me away. Stopping them from focussing, making them slow to turn, slow to notice. I have found that if I fight the urge to blink a film of tear forms, keeping the world at a distance.

Not that anyone seems to watch that carefully. I am sure this place is only a temporary ward, it feels half-finished, distracted, as if the people here have something more important they wish to be getting back to. The few people there are. Sometimes it is hard to find a nurse at all and they are always rushing, always looking tired. It must be like this everywhere, because of the earthquake. It makes it easier for me. It is only the Doctor I have to fear, and as far as I can tell the doctors only come in once a day, usually in the evening or at night, to hurry through their rounds.

So I took to walking, and it was such a relief to be out of the room that I had to be careful not to let a smile show. Along the corridors, lapping the ward. Past the nurses' station, then the toilets, through the day room where visitors sit with patients, trying to pretend they don't smell the piss in the air, trying not to watch the television. On to the rows of rooms, with our names written on cardboard tags, in case we forget. Only mine says Chris, a name someone has made up for me, and I'm not telling them any different. I'm not telling them anything. Walking and watching, because it beats doing nothing.

Then on my third lap I didn't turn. It was as if part of me was trying to run away. To leave all of this. To pick up a phone, talk, listen to a voice I know again, leave behind my unfinished business. I walked out through the doors as if I wasn't a patient at all, just some guy called in to check the wiring, wearing hospital pyjamas. Out past the deserted reception, beyond the lifts and the stairwell, understanding the danger but feeling lighter with each forbidden step. I could only go so far though. Fate has bound me here.

I saw a door which looked interesting, with a small glass window I couldn't see through, because the other side was so dimly lit. I was surprised to find it unlocked and walked through to a short dark corridor, ending in an exposed concrete wall. I just stood there and breathed in the musty dampness, pretending I was someplace else, pretending I was nowhere. For a moment I relaxed.

There were two doors leading off from the corridor. One said Cleaning and was locked. The other said Boiler and I opened it. It let me into this room. It's not a proper boiler room, just a space where the valves and switches regulating the heating in this wing of the hospital are. A small space, just room enough for someone checking the equipment to move around, and not enough air. There is a small fold-up chair. Perhaps I am not the only one who escapes here. It reminds me of a cupboard we used to have at home, where I used to go to draw when I was little. That's what made me think of writing. I had seen an exercise book in the waiting room and went back to get it. I found a pen in the reception area and walked back here with both stuffed down the back of my pyjamas. I am sure no one saw me.

As soon as I began the words came on in a rush, a rush of remembering, a rush of relief. Writing it down will keep me sane, in this time of waiting and plotting his death. And it will help me to order my memories, which are still liquid when I try to grasp them, turned to slush by the drugs.

I have another reason for writing this. It is my backup, in case I fail. I am going to post a letter to myself, at the school. I am hoping that if I never make it back, if the Doctor wins, someone will think to open it. It tells them where they can find this book, in the cavity of the wall behind the board I have managed to pull back, where I leave it hidden each day. So if I write it down, all of it, everything that happened, then even if I can not kill him, there is a chance the world will know what he has done. But that is a small consolation, a poor second best, and I don't want to think about it now.

I should tell what little I know about how I came to be here. I remember the five days up in the bush after the earthquake, but they are part of the Doctor's story and I will write them separately to keep this in order. What happened later is less clear and mostly I am guessing. I must have been found by somebody and brought here, to Palmerston North, the closest hospital still standing. I was injured, concussed perhaps, exhausted, and badly dehydrated. But this is not a ward for the physically broken, instead I take my sleep each night amongst the mentally disturbed. The Doctor must have seen me come in. He must have felt so lucky, that the only witness fell into his hands this way. Then he found some excuse to have me transferred, it can't have been too difficult amongst the mayhem. And he prescribed me the cocktail of drugs that I'm sure were meant to take my mind away. That's the way I figure it anyway. A simple plan, or just the first step, while he decides how to deal with me.

Only something went wrong, something I don't understand. Somehow I stopped taking the pills. I don't know how. I wish I did. All these empty spaces in my head frighten me. It could have been an accident I suppose, the pills knocked to the floor when a nurse's back was turned. However it happened I have been set free. It was like slowly coming awake after a long sleep, still half-trapped in dreams. All the surroundings both familiar and strange, as if I had slept the whole time with my eyes open. Memories from the bush broke over me, and with them came the waking nightmares, all I have seen, the Doctor's face at the centre of it always. The nightmare sits here still, just below the surface of my thoughts, revealing itself in part each time they move.

I remember lying awake all through the night, trying to make some sense of the jumble, trying not to scream. Then the nurse came round that morning, pushing her trolley right through the middle of my panic.

'Morning silent Chris,' she chirped, not looking me in the eye, as if she knew there was nothing to be seen there. 'Have a good night did we?' She continued to chat as she took my pulse and my temperature, and while she did it I made my decision. It just seemed easier, safer, to stay quiet, flood my mind with nothingness, stare straight ahead, give nothing away. But not that easy. There was a part of me that wanted to break down sobbing, cling to her, ask her all the questions that float without answers, ask her to tell me impossible things, tell me everything will be alright. Instinct stopped me.

That evening, after two more visits from the trolley, two more rounds of pretending to swallow, I saw the Doctor and no sight could have brought more certainty. Instinct had saved my life.

Now I will keep pretending. I will wait until the time is right and then, I will show the world that Marko Turner is not as useless as they all thought. I will make the Doctor pay.

4.

The challenge of the Coast to Coast was for the whole PE class to get itself from one side of the island to the other in under six days. The way Mr Camden introduced it to us the trip was entirely ours. We would plan the route, assess the risks, do the organisation, he was just there to observe. The way he did it was slightly different. Mr Camden isn't exactly the observing type and he couldn't resist dropping hints, guiding discussions, leading or prodding whenever he thought he could get away with it. We let him have his fun and by the end of term we had miraculously settled on the same basic itinerary classes had been using for the last fifteen years. We were to bus out to Riversdale and from there bike to the foothills of the Tararuas. We then gave ourselves three days to tramp across the ranges and planned to finish by rafting down the Otaki River with a full day to spare. Simple.

We met together early on the Friday morning, to load our bikes on to the support vehicle and distribute the food most groups had bought in a mad rush the night before. By then we were as prepared as we could be, in a last minute slack-arsed sort of a way. We'd covered all the theory in class but looking around the gym steps it was easy to see our practical skills were still lagging behind. Packs that wouldn't quite close, with bits hanging off the sides, tempting the elements. People repacking for the third time, the gear expanding with each attempt, glimpses of heavy clothes that would quickly waterlog and coats that would never withstand proper mountain rain.

It was the same with the bikes. I helped load up the trailer because I was nervous and it gave me something to do. There were perished tyres and rusting chains, brake cables only a couple of strands short of disaster. Maybe somebody watching would have thought we'd been poorly prepared but that wasn't true. They might have thought we just didn't care but that was wrong too, you could tell that just by listening in to the conversations that were starting, winding our nerves up, stretching them tighter.

'Piss off, you carry it.'

'I've already got the tent.'

'Well you find a place in here for it then. Go on. See, there's no room is there? Hey, what are you doing?'

'You don't need this.'

'Fuck off. I don't go through your stuff.'

'You won't find shit like this in it if you do.'

'No, that's mine.'

'And this is our tent. I think it's sort of a priority don't you?'

'Okay, but if I end up needing that I'm ...'

All of us feeling the same, wondering what it would be like to fail, and who we might blame if we did. Not that any of us had imaginations wild enough to pick what was waiting for us up in the hills.

The bus we'd hired arrived. I saw Jeremy, who'd been in charge of booking it, breathe out with relief. It was bigger than we needed, just eighteen students divided into four expedition groups, and Mr Camden. The other three adults were taking a car over but not him. He couldn't bear to be that far from the action. He bounded up the stairs, last on, and stood there beaming down on us. He pretended to be doing a head count but that wasn't his job. I knew he was just taking the chance to soak it all in: his latest recruits. He thought about giving one of his little speeches, I saw his lips moving in preparation, but the bus shuddered into life just in time. We were off. It had started.

The journey took just over three hours. At first we tried to make like it was any other bus ride, sitting with our mates, hanging our conversations over the backs of seats, arguing about whatever music people tried to pass up to the driver. But then, within half an hour of leaving and without anyone having to suggest it, we'd moved into our expedition groups and the talk had turned to distances and menus. Anxious conversations with people carefully laying lines of blame, in case it all went wrong.

My group was definitely the worst. In theory the class had been split according to ability but there had been a lot of chopping and changing since then. I'm the sort who prefers to keep his opinions to himself which is how I found myself dragged along by the social currents, washed up with the group of leftovers.

Officially we were the 'middle slow group' and we sat near the front on the driver's side, all of us thinking the same thing, how the other three weren't the first people we'd choose to spend six days of our lives with. Jonathon's the easiest of the other three to describe so I'll start with him. He had a special skill which was well known to everybody, the skill of pissing other people off. It doesn't sound much, said like that, but Jonathon had it down to an art form. He was like one of those natural athletes you see who never seems to train but still excels at everything. Jonathon could get right in under your skin without appearing to try. The first time I saw him in action Mr Camden was his victim. It was at the beginning of the year, only two weeks into the course.

We were doing our orienteering practical, the first assessment. There was a course we had to negotiate through the pine plantation behind the school. I'd completed mine earlier in the week and I was at the end with Mr Camden, helping him to record finishing times. Jonathon was the first person into view, with only one checkpoint left and plenty of time in hand. He's fit enough and too devious to be stupid. As soon as he saw us he stopped jogging and ambled over, like we were friends he'd bumped into during a weekend bush walk. He knew the stopwatch was still on, just like he knew the time would determine his final grade.

'Hi guys. There you go.' He handed Mr Camden his clipboard, where all the checkpoint numbers got marked off.

'You've still got one to get there Jonathon,' Mr Camden pointed out, just like he was meant to.

'That's alright. Think I'll stop here.' Jonathon gave a shrug and smiled.

'What do you mean? There's one marker left. You're on course for a level six. Away you go.'

'But what grade do I get if I just stop now?' Jonathon asked, all innocent. Mr Camden stared at him as if he couldn't even begin to understand the question.

'One more in under three minutes and you get the top grade. Hurry up. The watch is still on.'

'Grade three isn't it, if I fail to complete by one marker?' Jonathon kept pushing.

'You can see the marker from here for God's sake. Do it or there's no grade at all.' Just like that. Mr Camden had snapped. With Jonathon you don't even see it coming.

'You can't do that. I'd appeal. Here, I'm quite happy with a three. Three's a pass, the way I see it.' He tapped the clipboard and sauntered off and I watched the red rise in Mr Camden's face. He never forgave Jonathon for that. He singled him out whenever he could and even tried to get him moved out of the class. Of course that just made Jonathon happier, because that's the way he is. Not exactly the type I'd choose to help me slog my way across the country. I spent a lot of that bus trip watching him, wondering how long it would take him to find a way in through my soft defences.

Then there was Rebecca, who should never have been in a group like ours. Four days before she had been a major player in the élite group, who were planning to complete the whole journey in only four days. She was fit and she was popular. Her dad tutored some outdoor pursuits course at a local polytech. But even people like Rebecca can slip up. She was meant to be going out with a guy called Shannon Robertson, who wasn't in our class but was best mates with the other people in her group. So when it got out that she'd been seen going off with some guy from Coll at a party on the weekend the group became outraged on Shannon's behalf. She was no longer welcome amongst them and was banished to the furthest reaches of the class. We were her punishment. There's probably more to it but that sort of gossip has a way of finding its way around people like me. What I do know is that Christina Meade, who I'd half-considered making a move on during the trip, was promoted, and Rebecca, who sort of scared me, moved in. On the trip over the hill I could see she was caught between two moods, half-wanting to take over and show us all the things we were doing wrong, half-trapped inside her sulk, determined to remain quiet and miserable.

Lisa is harder to describe from back then. I knew least about her. I don't think anyone in the class knew her much. She was new that year. She'd transferred over from some private girls' school, and she didn't seem to have made many friends. It was hard to know whether she was quiet because she was new, or whether she'd always been that way. Even after ten weeks together people would often pause before saying her name, like they were using it for the first time and frightened of getting it wrong.

And of course there was me. I wonder what the others would have said about Marko Turner then, if you asked them. Quiet too, probably, and a little bit soft. They'll think differently, when the Doctor is dead.

5.

April 18

I wasn't able to write yesterday. It was too risky, getting to the room.

I have seen the Doctor again. Last night I woke to find him standing beside me, his hand on my wrist, checking my pulse. It took all my control not to let out a scream, or reach out and take his neck in my hands. Somehow I managed to stop myself, force my eyes to flicker without recognition, closing again while I slowly counted out my breathing, trying to stop my pulse from racing. I heard him walk to the end of my bed and check my charts and all the time I felt the hatred swirling up inside of me, mixing wildly with my fear. Then I heard him walk away. I took a risk and opened my eyes again. He was still out in the corridor, talking to a nurse. About me I bet. About my medication.

Whatever it is he thinks I'm taking it must be strong. Four days without it has not been enough to clear my head. There are times when my eyesight goes fuzzy and I can only write this in small bursts, before the words lose shape.

There have been three different nurses bringing my pills round so far. Two of them don't worry me at all. They're always rushing and don't seem to notice much. It's easy enough to slip the pills under my tongue, I don't even have to pretend to swallow. The third is called Margaret and Margaret is different. She is older, about my mother's age, only unlike my mother there's not much she misses. Last night, after she had handed over the little paper cup with the three pills rattling inside, she stopped and stared me down. I looked away, like I hadn't noticed, but still I could feel her eyes on me, not moving until the cup was handed back empty and I had finished the glass of water she'd given me. It is as if she knows but she isn't saying, doesn't want to give anything away. Neither do I.

I took a chance coming here today. I knew another day without writing could break me. There was someone standing in the nurses' station but they were busy reading from a folder and I hurried past, head down, hoping they wouldn't notice. Then I ran, as best I could, so even if they followed I might lose them. I decided to wait here a while before I got this book out, just in case. Being careful is second nature now.

When the door opened part of me was expecting it. I'd tried to lock it but that needed a key. I had sat down on the chair and brought my knees up beneath my chin, trying to look harmless and crazy. I am lucky it was only Andrew, one of the orderlies. They must have been too busy and sent him out to look. I don't know how he knew to try in here. He's one of the better ones around here, as far as I can tell. He's always smiling, no matter who he's dealing with — some up themselves doctor or a patient who's losing it. Not that I trust him. I don't trust anyone here, not until it's done.

So when he smiled at me I didn't smile back. I didn't move.

'You alright?' he asked and I didn't respond. I willed him to leave it there, to walk away. He had to think about it, and in the wait our silence grew larger.

'Okay, just our little secret then,' he whispered and I had to bite my tongue hard to stop the relief from spreading over my face. He shut the door behind him when he left and I moved the chair so I was sitting up against it. That was forty-five minutes ago and still no one has come so I figure it's safe now to be doing this.

6.

Riversdale isn't a town. It's a name on the map where the rugged east coast of the Wairarapa relaxes just long enough to become a beach, a beach where baches have collected about a single shop, a camp site, and a golf course. There're sixty kilometres of winding road before you reach Masterton, through land where drought calls every year and windless days are marked down on a calendar. Sheep country turning to pine, hilly enough to prompt nervous cycling talk as we watched out the bus windows.

We stayed a kilometre or so back from the beach in accommodation originally built for shearers. The small cabins formed a U-shape around an area of grass. Off to one side was a kitchen and two outside toilets. Basic stuff but 'the most luxury you'll being seeing this week so enjoy it', Mr Camden delighted in telling us. Enjoying it meant stretching out in the sun and pretending this was the beginning of a holiday, and hoping someone else would volunteer to do dinner.

Ours was the last group to organise itself. It was the only

night we had access to an oven and like everyone else we'd opted for simple food, two large frozen pizzas thawing messily somewhere amongst our gear.

'So how's our dinner going then?' Jonathon finally asked as the other groups started to emerge from the kitchen with plates of steaming food.

'It isn't my job,' Rebecca told him.

'Didn't say it was.'

Lisa was lying on the grass with her pack as a pillow, pretending to be asleep. I did the same, even though I was hungry. Ms Jenkins, our assigned adult, was with us. We were meant to be feeding her too. I'm sure she wanted to get up and do it herself but she had to sit back and observe. They were the rules. We'd talked about her on the bus but none of us had been in any of her classes. She taught Science and Jonathon thought she might have been his little brother's form teacher. She was quite young, only in her second year, and she'd seemed shy when she'd introduced herself to the class the previous week.

'So you're so hungry, you do it,' Rebecca said.

'Didn't say I was hungry either,' Jonathon told her.

'Fine. Neither am I.'

'Ah, I think Mr Camden wants to do the briefing at eight,' Ms Jenkins reminded us. We ignored her, not because we were trying to be rude but because we were ignoring each other too, none of us wanting to give in, in case that set the trend for the rest of the trip. Rebecca broke first.

'You're all useless!' She stood up and made a great show

of rummaging through the bags. She located the pizzas and stormed off into the kitchen. When she came back a minute later I saw her look around us all, waiting for someone to say thanks. Nobody did and that really pissed her off. She took her logbook from her pack and scribbled angrily into it. Jonathon sat cross-legged and rolled a cigarette. Ms Jenkins sat awkwardly on the one picnic table in the middle of the grass. I went back to pretending to be asleep. I think by then Lisa really was. We waited.

'So how's our pizza?' Jonathon asked again, twenty minutes later.

'How should I know?' Rebecca replied.

'Shouldn't you check then?'

'I put it in. You check.'

'How long ago was that?' I asked, realising too late the game Rebecca was playing. Just then a window opened above us and two charred disks, still smoking, were hurled out on to the grass, accompanied by laughter from within.

'Shit,' Jonathon said. 'You've burnt them.'

'Me? How was it me?' Rebecca managed to sound both indignant and triumphant.

'It was a reasonable thing to assume,' Jonathon told her.

'For someone too lazy to get off their fat arse maybe.'

'You'd better cook us something else then,' Jonathon said.

'You cook it.'

'Already told you, I'm not hungry. Anyway, I've lined up some of the pasta Andrew's group had.'

'Well what about one of these two sleeping beauties then?'

Rebecca said, pointing at Lisa and me in turn. 'This is supposed to be a group you know.'

'She does have a point,' Ms Jenkins offered. That shamed me into speaking, even though I didn't want to get involved in any of Jonathon's games.

'There's some extra bread for tonight, and cheese,' I said. 'I could make some toasted sandwiches.'

'It talks,' Jonathon mocked.

'I'll help then,' Lisa added blearily. 'Come on.'

Only we'd run out of time. Mr Camden had decided he wanted to hold the briefing early and wouldn't let us back into the kitchen. We were forced to sit in one corner of the communal lounge, sharing round bread and cheese and accusing stares while better smells hung in the air. In amongst a room of excited chatter we were the one pocket of disgruntled silence. Rebecca was the most irritated, even though she did her best to hide it from the gloating élite group. I could see Jonathon getting happier by the minute, feeding off her misery.

Mr Camden made us go through our plans for the next day. The first group were planning to leave early and have the 100 kilometre cycle leg completed by two o'clock, giving them time to tramp over to Cone Hut before dark. The rest of us were leaving at a more decent hour, aiming only to make it to the shelter at the Waiohine road end.

Each group had its own little cabin, an arrangement the rest of the class had decided upon. Once again we were victim to the rule of remainders. Although we put it off as long as possible, eventually we were forced to come together in the small room. There was barely space for the bunks and only one window which was jammed shut. We got it open after much combined grunting, letting in a swarm of mosquitoes and setting off another round of accusations. That should have been enough trouble for one night but Jonathon was indefatigable. While the rest of us claimed our beds he decided it would be a good time to go through his gear. He took his pack, upended it and shook the contents free onto the small space at his feet.

'What are you doing?' Rebecca snapped, straight off. Me and her had taken the two top bunks and from her vantage point she could see the sorry state of his gear.

'Repacking.'

'Look at your stuff. Is that how you're going to do it?'

'What's it to you?'

'Where's your packliner?'

'Don't need one.'

'Until it rains.'

'It's all in plastic.' They could have made a documentary out of it, the way he was winding her up. His gear surrounded him in small clumps, tied up in supermarket bags, pretty much exactly as we'd been told not to do it.

'You know they're no good,' Rebecca said. 'Water'll get in the top.'

'Not your problem,' Jonathon shrugged.

'I'm not tramping with you if you're this badly prepared.'

'Whatever.' Lisa and I remained silent on the sideline.

'Oh for God's sake, these'll rip. Look!' Exasperated, Rebecca leapt from her bunk, grabbed the nearest package and swung it wildly above her. As intended the bag gave way, sending the contents flying. It would have been quite an effective demonstration, if she hadn't by chance chosen his underwear bag. A pair of bright yellow boxers with a smiling face landed neatly on her head and it was impossible not to laugh. That was the scene Ms Jenkins walked in on. She stood silently in the doorway, looking as if she didn't know quite what to make of it.

'Ah Rebecca,' she said. 'You really shouldn't use those bags. They're not very waterproof.' That set us off again.

'I'm perfectly aware of that, thank you,' Rebecca fumed and hauled herself back up on to her bunk.

'Well I suppose if you're sure. Ah, Jonathon, here's the packliner you ordered.' She passed him the bright orange bag and backed out of the room. 'See you all in the morning.'

'You're something of a prick aren't you Jonathon?' I observed when she had left.

'Do my best.'

Lisa suggested we check through our food again, as we'd decided earlier, but Rebecca, probably fearing another ambush, refused to co-operate. I wriggled into my sleeping bag that night certain we'd got off to the worst possible start. It was going to get much worse.

7.

April 19

Already it feels as if I've been acting too long. It's like being trapped underwater, your body dying to let go of the stale air, your mind struggling against it. I've heard when you're drowning there's a point where you let the fight go, slip away without even realising. The body wins in the end. Last night it almost happened to me. I was in the toilets, with the door locked behind me, when I heard a strange sound fingering the walls of the cubicle. It took me a second to realise it was my own voice.

'I am Marko,' I was mumbling. 'I am Marko.' Like my head was so full of unspoken words they were starting to overflow. Even when I realised, it was a battle to make myself stop. It felt so good, making those sounds, tickling the scratch that's been itching my mind so long. Only the thought of the Doctor, and all the things I owe him, kept me silent.

Today was more pretending. I walk all the time now and nobody seems to pay me much attention. 'This isn't who I am' plays continuously in my head but it hardly helps. Half the people in here would tell you they were sane, if you asked them. Sometimes the doctors agree. They come around with the news and the discharge papers, and a solemn handshake to underline the importance of the occasion. Then the family arrive, familiar from visiting time, masks of relief slipped over uncertain faces. Not me though. The good Doctor has other plans for Marko Turner.

I've been allowed to join the craft therapy class. It's not the sort of thing I'd usually bother with but in a day full of nothing a trip to the toilet can be a highlight. We're making leather belts. It's easy enough, although I'm careful not to cope too well. It is difficult, not knowing what is expected of me. They provide the strips of leather and there are three stencils to choose from, for hammering in the designs, and punches to make the holes. It is a statement of trust, letting us near so many sharp instruments. Today Billy gave them pause for thought.

I didn't provoke him. Why would I? I was working on my third belt, happily lost in the simple task. I suppose I just looked up at the wrong moment, when his big clumsy fingers were having trouble threading the buckle through the loop he'd closed way too tight. Big fingers on huge hands, out of place at the end of his thin unremarkable arms. He'd be in his forties I guess, bald with a red nose and a desk worker's stomach. He's got a family, a wife and two kids who visit most days. I have a game here where I try to fit patients to their stories, imagine what finally pushed them out of the zone. With Billy it's the hands I keep coming back to. It would get anyone eventually, having hands that weren't your own. I've got small hands, same as my mum. Maybe Billy saw them, and how I'd already finished two belts. Maybe that pissed him off. Or it could be that being crazy means you don't need much in the way of reasons.

One thing I'll say for being in here, it's done wonders for my reactions. Normally I doubt I'd have spotted him moving so early. It gave me time to step aside, so his big lunge took him straight past me. He crashed against the table where a previous group's papier mâché was displayed. He turned to face me again and all the anger I've been sitting on rose up to meet him. Suddenly it wasn't Billy in front of me, it was the Doctor. Without thinking I had hold of both his shoulders and with a force I didn't know I could muster I had crashed him back against the wall. My face drew close to his and I felt how easy it would be to kill him. Only it wasn't the Doctor, it was just poor Billy, and all my rage was useless.

'Want some do ya?' I almost hissed into his poor bewildered face. He'd already forgotten how this had happened. I stopped myself. Stared through him the way I hoped a crazy who's done with talking might stare. Then I slowly backed away.

It was the right call. Margaret was our supervisor and as I turned I saw how closely she was watching me, looking for some sign. She knows something, I'm sure of it. Maybe she has followed me to this room. Maybe Andrew told her. I've taken a thread from my pyjamas and I'm going to leave it stretched across the place where I hide this writing, so I can be sure no one is reading it. It's not paranoia, it's good sense. They're the same thing, when you've seen the things I've seen.

8.

We left just before nine-thirty the next morning, after loading our packs on to the support vehicle trailer. Joe Stewart, a huge man with three chins, who 'used to enjoy this sort of thing myself before my back went' was the driver. His son had done the expedition a few years earlier and so he let us use his time and his big four-wheel drive for free. Ours was the second to last group to leave, Mr Camden's idea. I think he was scared if he let us go last he'd never see us again.

'Now don't worry,' he told us as we biked past the gate and out on to the road. 'I've been doing this fifteen years and no group's ever failed to complete the cycle leg.' He should have known someone like Jonathon was always going to take that as a challenge.

A week earlier Mr Camden had brought a guest speaker into the class, a woman he knew who'd once cycled in the Commonwealth Games. She explained how the effort on a bike could be minimised by riding as a pack, cutting down the wind resistance. Her promise of being able to reduce energy output by a third captured our short-cutting imaginations.

It seemed so simple when we were sitting behind our desks, free from real life complications. Complications like Jonathon.

Him and Rebecca started out in front, with me and Lisa tucked in behind and Ms Jenkins at the back. Straight away he was looking for ways to make it awkward for us. He hit on the idea of setting an impossible-to-follow rhythm, taking off in little bursts and then slowing to the point where we had to brake to avoid hitting him. Rebecca tried to match the pace, she's stubborn that way, but behind them we were struggling, the way he'd intended. I could feel my legs already burning with the uneven pace, exactly the thing we'd been told to avoid. The trip proper was only thirty minutes old and already Jonathon had his first victory. He'd made group riding inefficient.

Despite this we made reasonable time, covering the first thirty kilometres in just over an hour and a half. Then the day's only real hill loomed and Jonathon, sensing we were near breaking, couldn't resist. He stood up out of his saddle and put in a huge burst. Rebecca didn't miss a beat and matched him pedal for pedal, pushing him on even harder. I spend quite a bit of time mucking around on my bike and maybe I could have kept with them if I'd really tried, but after a morning at Lisa's side a sort of loyalty was forming. It surprised me to see Ms Jenkins glide past us both, hardly puffing, trying hard not to look too pleased with herself.

'I hate that prick,' Lisa muttered, staring straight ahead over her handlebars. Her face was red and shiny with sweat and her helmet had slipped down over her forehead.

'I reckon,' I gasped back. They were the first words we'd spoken all morning and it was all it took for us to become friends.

When we reached the top the other three were waiting on the side of the road, trying to look relaxed although their faces still glowed with their efforts.

'Come on Lisa,' Jonathon taunted, as if he could tell the silence had already been broken. 'You're holding us up.'

'She's doing just fine,' I said, too quickly.

'Oh yes, a little bond developing is there Marko?' Johnny asked. Behind him Rebecca smirked.

'Fuck you arsehole,' Lisa snapped. 'You're the one not doing your job.'

'I don't think that's fair Lisa,' Ms Jenkins said, trying to stop an argument. She was too late. The match had been struck and we were all in the mood to throw on some petrol. Abuse built quickly upon accusation, loyalties dissolving as quickly as the next insult could be conjured. By the time Mr Camden's group arrived, fifteen minutes later, there was no group left, just four pissed off individuals and a teacher who must have wished she'd stayed at home.

Mr Camden tried his best to sort things out, suggesting me and Lisa take a turn at the front. Then he took his group off ahead. I don't think he was all that keen on being there when his great idea fell apart. It did. Jonathon and Rebecca sat right on our back wheels the whole way, complaining about the pace, and the more they complained the slower

Lisa went. Then, to add to the fun, Lisa and Jonathon punctured and I broke my chain changing gear on a hill. They were the sort of things that could have been fixed quickly enough, by a group that was co-operating, or at least still talking to one another. Instead we sniped and obstructed and found ourselves a full hour and a half behind schedule at the next stop, a point Jonathon was quick to seize upon.

'Putting you two in the front has really done wonders then hasn't it?'

'At least we're keeping the group together,' Lisa replied.

'Together in fucken Riversdale,' Rebecca muttered.

'It would have been faster walking.'

'You can't plan for mechanical breakdowns,' Ms Jenkins tried. 'I think we're doing very well.'

For some reason that got to Lisa even more than Jonathon's digs. She took her bike by the seat stem and, pivoting on her heels, swung it about her like a hammer thrower. It sailed an impressive distance down the road then bounced a few metres more.

'No!' she screamed at us all. 'We are not doing very well at all. In fact, we're doing very fucken badly.' She stared at us, daring us to speak. Then she turned and headed back down the road, in the direction we had come.

'Aren't you going to go with her then?' Jonathon smirked at me. Ms Jenkins seemed less amused.

'Lisa!' she called out, proper impatience edging into her voice for the first time. Only one day together and already she was sick of us. Lisa turned, hands on hips.

'I'm going to take a shit. Does anyone have a problem with that?'

We waited in awkward silence. I sat in the grass and tried to ignore the others. Jonathon had a go at winding Rebecca up but she didn't respond. Ms Jenkins retrieved Lisa's bike and pretended to check it for damage. In the time it took Lisa to relieve herself, and do some crying too judging by her eyes when she got back, we all of us lost the will to pedal. We stopped even pretending to ride in formation, overtaking and dropping back in random patterns of fading energy. The whole time Ms Jenkins hovered in the background, like a nervous sheepdog too afraid to bark. The only time any of us opened our mouths it was to spit out a bug or complain. We'd planned on making Masterton by lunchtime. It was half-past two before we even reached the outskirts. The support vehicle was waiting there for us, to check everything was alright.

'Not too long now,' Joe Stewart lied, leaning out the Pajero window. He had a way of smiling at nothing, like the rest of the world was slow to get the joke. 'Any problems here?'

'Having the time of our lives thanks Joe,' Jonathon told him, dripping sarcasm although in his case I think he was quite enjoying it. Either way Joe wasn't one for hidden messages.

'Righty-ho then, see you up the river.' He was gone before any of us could think of a way of stopping him.

'What did you say that for?' Rebecca demanded.

'What, so you're not having fun then?' Jonathon smiled. 'Sorry, must have misread the mood.'

'We could have got a ride,' Lisa said.

'At least the worst bit's over,' Ms Jenkins tried, but that was so lame we didn't even bother arguing.

A three-two vote took us to McDonalds for lunch. We figured we were already riding so badly a bit of crap food wasn't going to make it any worse. And it's reliable crap, the sort you can take comfort in when nothing else is going to plan. There's even something comforting about the surroundings, flecked tables with wooden borders, the photos of spotty employees-of-the-month on the wall and Ronald staring madly at you from the children's play area. And there's the smell of the place, the odour of hot grease floating above industrial strength disinfectant. Hell, it's like coming home. Maybe that explains the way we started to relax. Somewhere in amongst stealing each other's fries and complaining about the ice, we forgot we were fighting. Conversations even started.

'I don't even know why I took PE,' Lisa told us, dipping the crust of her cheese burger into my sauce. 'The whole thing sucks.'

'Reckon,' Rebecca said, instead of taking the chance to attack.

'You know,' Jonathon announced, the first sparkle of a plan already alight in his sick little eyes, 'Mr Camden will be spewing if we don't make the campsite tonight.'

I saw the simple genius of it immediately. It was an idea

whose time had come. I reminded them of Mr Camden's earlier challenge.

'Fifteen years and no one's ever failed.'

'What are you suggesting?' Ms Jenkins asked, looking worried.

'Not suggesting anything,' Jonathon replied, standing and sucking in his stomach. 'Just thinking I might go another dessert, that's all.'

We all followed him up to the counter. I was full and almost out of money but that wasn't the point. It just felt good to finally all be headed in the same direction.

The longer we lingered over the sugar the more frequently Ms Jenkins checked her watch.

'So what exactly are you planning to do?' she finally asked.

'Simple,' Jonathon told her, happily speaking on all our behalves. 'We push on until it gets dark, then we find a place to camp for the night.' He said it casually, between chewing his last mouthful, like it was the most sensible thing in the world. It wasn't. All our gear was in the support vehicle to start with. We didn't have any food and stopping short of the road end would only make the next day longer. It went against all our safety guidelines and we would probably fail the trip assignment on the strength of it. No one said any of those things though. There was too much incentive not to. We were never going to make a success of the day but here Jonathon was offering us the chance to be outstanding in our failure. Ms Jenkins wanted to tell us we were wrong but she couldn't. It was our trip and they were the rules.

Lisa and Jonathon still had money left and walked round the corner to buy food for the night. Then it was back on the bikes and the irony of our call quickly became clear. The new sense of purpose had fuelled our legs and it was obvious we were making the best time of the day. It would be an exaggeration to say we'd all become friends but there had been a definite thawing. There were even the beginnings of conversation jumping between riders, like little bursts of static electricity.

An hour later the road we'd been following into the hills turned to gravel. We had reached the point where the dark green of the Tararuas' spreading fingers touched the farmland of the plains. The sun had already dipped behind the hills, making them cold and unwelcoming. Below us to our right the Waiohine River snaked darkly out of its gorge. A signpost told us we were only nine kilometres from reaching the others.

'We'll make it from here easily,' Ms Jenkins told us. Even allowing for fatigue and the way the road ahead rose and fell through the valley she was right. We had a good hour before it would get properly dark. Jonathon however had other ideas.

'Let's camp down there.' He pointed to an old barn near the river, half-obscured by a stand of pines.

'Why?' Ms Jenkins asked. 'Your food's up there, your sleeping bags, all of your gear.'

'And debriefs,' Jonathon replied. 'More lectures, more

planning, the other groups.' I knew what he was saying. The day hadn't been perfect but it was improving. It would be a shame to ruin it.

'If it's the riding you're tired of,' Ms Jenkins tried to reason, 'I'm sure we could just wait here a while. They're sure to send Joe back, if we're not there by dark.'

'No, sorry. Group decision. Come on.' Jonathon heaved his bike up over the fence and looked to the rest of us for support. One by one we followed him, leaving Ms Jenkins on the other side, alone and with no choice at all.

'Well whose barn is it? We should at least ask. There was a house, just back there on the right. Would you like me to check?'

But we were already moving, the group taking control, making our own decisions, just like we'd been told to. It felt good.

So did the barn. It was an old wooden building with a row of tiny windows high up on one side. Years earlier it would have started life as a shearing shed. It was empty apart from a small stack of rectangular bales in one corner, reaching halfway up the wall. The darkness was thick with smells; hay and cowshit, tractor oil and rust, and the dank trapped-air scent of cobwebs in black corners. We wheeled our bikes in with us, for security reasons Jonathon said, although it was more that none of us wanted to be spotted.

Lisa and me had our coats with us. We lay them on the ground and the food was dumped on top. It was a feast of convenience; two big bags of chips, a loaf of bread, bananas, two two-litre Cokes and a Chupa Chup each. Food guaranteed to corrode bad moods. Soon Ms Jenkins was laughing along with us and taking her swigs from the communal bottles.

We retired early to our 'bedroom', the flat top of the hay-stack. We were forced to lie close in the small space and soon we were warm beneath a single layer of conversation. It was the sort of talk you always get, when half-strangers open up. Stories most of it, trying to impress each other with things we'd done and people we knew. After that come new stories, to make people laugh, with the joke turned on the teller because you know it doesn't matter too much.

Lisa got into it most. Quiet Lisa. Suddenly we couldn't shut her up, like she'd slipped out in the darkness and some-one else had taken her place. She told us about the private school her father had made her attend, because he was afraid of the damage boys might do. I thought how he might have reacted if he could have seen her then, sandwiched between me and Jonathon on the top of some stranger's stack of hay.

Ms Jenkins mostly listened but later when the questions turned her way she let a few things out, surprising things like how she'd lived in Africa when she was little or worked a year as a tour bus driver in the South Island.

Jonathon, when he talked, tried to bring the conversa-tion back to the present, I think because the whole barn thing had been his idea. We talked about the others, camped up the end, being made to get an early night's sleep, and how pissed off Mr Camden would be when he saw us the next morning.

Pissed off but determined not to let it show, as it happened. It was just after eight o'clock and we were already on the road. We saw the Pajero's dustball running down through the valley and pulled over to await our bollocking. I watched Ms Jenkins's face tighten as Mr Camden climbed down from the passenger seat. She was one of us now, another naughty little teenager.

I was expecting a lecture but it didn't happen. Maybe he didn't trust himself, once he got started. Instead it was straight into the questions, disapproval dressed up as formality.

'Where did you sleep last night?'

'In a barn,' Jonathon replied, sounding quite pleased with himself. 'Worth noting for future years actually, it was very comfortable.'

'You missed your seven-thirty radio sked.'

'Radio's with our gear. We thought you might have done it for us.' And just then Mr Camden would have liked to hit him, the way people often do. But there are laws, and jobs to consider, so he turned away and addressed the rest of his questions directly at Ms Jenkins, even though that meant breaking his own rules.

'So your plans from here have altered have they?'

'Yeah. I think they just want to do Cone tonight, Alpha tomorrow and then over the top and down to Parawai Tuesday.'

'If nothing else goes wrong,' he added, like she was stupid not to have said it herself. There was a lot more he would have liked to say but he didn't even try. 'Your gear's up at the road end. If you're not there by nine Mr Stewart has been instructed to leave without your bikes.'

'Sweet as Mr C,' Jonathon called after him. 'Good seeing you.'

We rode off and Joe Stewart winked at us as we passed, like he'd seen it all before.

We did make it by nine, but only just. The other groups had already left and we took our time loading up the bikes, so there'd be no chance of catching them. Then we hauled on our packs for the first time and said all the obvious things.

'Okay, who put the rocks in here?'

'You think yours is heavy. Try this one.'

'There's no way me and this pack are going up that mountain.'

'Do you think we could just head straight down to the river and float out?'

'Do packs float?'

'It'd take us to the wrong coast.'

'Actually I think it goes to the lake.'

'Actually I don't care. I'm not walking up there.'

'Come on, let's get going. It'll seem better once we've started.'

'No, it'll seem better after a cigarette. Wait a sec.'

Eventually we got moving. First up was a one-at-a-time wire swing bridge suspended high above the gorge. The view from the middle took my mind off the weight of my pack, for a second or two anyway. There was something awesome about the determined progress of the water below, and the path it had cut through the solid rock walls. Above them was the thick bush we were headed into.

We'd been warned the first climb, up on to the ridge running along the eastern side of the Waiohine Valley, was one of the steepest of the trip. At times we had to grab at tree roots and branches as our feet lost traction. My lungs burned in a new way, my legs hurt and I felt like throwing up. Luckily it was a short climb by Tararua standards, only an hour and a half before it flattened out, and that was with plenty of stops to share our complaints around. Although we all knew we could have pushed on to Alpha and caught up with the others, none of us mentioned it, not even Ms Jenkins.

We dawdled along the tops, where the bush became lighter and the mud was just deep enough to ooze in over the tops of our boots. When we reached the sign pointing down to Cone, Lisa produced a camera, like she'd known all along this would turn into a trip worth recording. It took three goes for her to master the self-take function. Then we hurtled down the steep descent. The thought of almost being there brought the conversations back, happy disjointed stuff like we'd been friends forever.

Cone Hut is old-style, built of thick slabs of totara on a terrace above the river. The inside is dark and dirty and it would take a decent storm to make it look inviting. We opted for the collapsed picnic table outside and lay out our lunch: a small banquet thanks to the food we should have eaten the night before.

We spent that afternoon hanging by the river, all of us mellowing, while the much-talked about Tararua wind left us pretty much alone. It was one of those days where you want to ask 'why can't life always be like this?' You don't though, because you know it's a stupid question. It just can't.

9.

April 20

Someone has left a radio here. It's small and plastic, just like the one Lewis carries, only yellow instead of orange. Maybe Andrew left it for me. He hasn't said anything to me, or checked in here again, but it could be his way of showing some kindness. Or it could be a trap. Someone checking, to see how much I understand. I found a station and then kept the sound right down low, so anyone listening outside wouldn't know. I had to press it hard against my ear to make out what was being said. I must have looked like a proper crazy then, all scrunched up in this chair, straining to catch the words, rocking backwards and forwards to stay warm.

The radio is still full of earthquake talk. It sounds like a total mess. At first just hearing the guy say 'Wellington' was almost too much. Thoughts of all the people back there, of what might have happened, of how badly I need to see them, ripped at my insides. But there's a thing I need to do first, a thing keeping me here.

They're saying the clean-up was a disaster in itself and people are starting to look for someone to blame. They're saying people should have been better prepared but that's not right. There's some things you can't be properly ready for, because being ready costs too much. Like dying.

The police are being criticised because it took so long for them to establish order but they had some guy on who said nobody had expected the looting. Apparently some people just went crazy, grabbing whatever they could, and when others tried to stop them it turned into a riot. And all the time people were still trapped beneath the collapsed buildings.

They talked about the gas explosions too, which I already knew about because we saw them from up on the ridge, huge silent flashes of mayhem. Then they had some professor trying to explain why so many people went wild. She said a lot of things but mostly she just told us that sometimes people can go a bit crazy. I already knew that too.

Now they say things are slowly returning to normal, or as close to normal as you can get in a city where so many have died that you have to ship in coffins from up north. The sort of normal that sees a lot of low-life crawling back beneath their rocks, trying to pretend the things they did never happened at all, in that time when craziness got out into the open. Doctors going back to being doctors, carefully cutting out the bits of the past that might infect them, stitching over the memories and hoping they might heal. Not my Doctor though. Not this wound. I can see him, better than he realises, and I am going to make him pay.

Then I turned off the radio and tried to let my hatred rise. It's the only way of keeping my mind off home, off Mum, who last time I saw her, when she dropped me off on her way to work, told me to be careful. Off Duncan, who has to be okay, because little brothers always are. Off so many people, each one a face that can weaken my resolve. I shouldn't even be writing this. I shouldn't let these thoughts in.

I have to think of useful things, I have to make plans. It isn't easy. I am still weak. A morning walking the wards exhausts me and writing this means pushing through the pain that thickens behind my eyes. Each morning I wake to see the world a little more clearly, but like a blind person learning to see, most of it only frightens me. And the things I don't see frighten me even more, people acting against me, staying just out of sight.

I am sure now that Margaret is dangerous. Today she came to my bed pushing her nurse's trolley, loaded up with all the usual things. She rummaged about in it for a while, for effect, then produced an unfriendly-looking syringe.

'Just need to take some blood,' she told me, wrapping a band around my arm and pulling it tight. 'To check how the medication levels are settling.' She may as well have said 'I'm on to you, you know.' She stared at me but I gave her nothing, and she gave me nothing back.

I followed her after she left, hanging in the background while she completed her rounds, watching her for clues. She is silent with some patients and chatty with others, the ones she thinks can understand. And she always chats to me. After the last room had been visited she wheeled her trolley back towards the nurses' station. I could hear the test tube, still warm with my blood, clanking against the side of a metal dish the whole way down the corridor. Then it stopped, just outside a door I always thought was a storeroom although it has no sign. I can not be certain, because her stopping there surprised me and I had to pull back into a doorway, but I think I saw her take my test tube and pocket it. She went in through the door and was back out almost immediately. Then she moved off.

I waited a good five minutes before I checked the room. It was home to three large wheelie bins, one marked 'biological refuse', the other two 'general'. Each had a small deposit slot at the top and was padlocked shut, so all I have are my suspicions. Suspicions that Margaret threw out my sample. So why would she do that? Reason is slow to reveal itself here. Maybe the sample wasn't ordered at all. Maybe she was just testing me, looking for a reaction. There must be other possibilities, possibilities I can't quite see, whose blurred, changing outlines keep me awake through the night.

10.

Sleep is the mind's way of shitting. Dreams are just thoughts you have no use for, thoughts that will poison you if you don't let them out. They say a lack of sleep will drive you crazy soon enough. None of us had slept much the night in the barn, three or four hours at most. The next night at Cone was even worse.

It's a small hut, no more than three metres by four. The sleeping space is a platform raised above the dirt floor where six people could lie comfortably, if there were mattresses. There weren't, unless you count one decaying lump of foam that smelt of dampness and grime and things you prefer not to imagine. We settled down early, straight after the radio sked. The weather report was for wind rising later the next day, and maybe some rain on the tops. We heard the other groups report in. All three of them were up at Alpha, so something must have held the fast group back. When the operator asked them if they had any messages they replied 'no thanks', as if we weren't even in the hills with them. That suited us fine. We didn't give any messages either. We wouldn't have to see them again until the end of the trip.

Lying down on the bare boards I could tell sleep was going to be difficult. I had that half-sick camp feeling you get – too much dried food, too much breathing in smoke from the open fire and a long drop not designed for relaxation. My stomach was tight, my throat was dry, and my mind was restless. I propped myself up on one elbow and looked around to see whether anyone else was feeling the same. Lisa was already sitting up. We both tried our best to get a conversation going, like it had been in the barn, but it was pointless. That mood had passed. We circled awkwardly for a while; school, family, childhood pets, before Jonathon put us out of our misery.

'Fuck up will you both? I'm trying to get some sleep here.'

I lay back down and dug my head into a pillow of track pants and polar fleece and waited for sleep to rescue me from the feeling of disappointment. The rats came first.

I was on the end, up against the wall. There was a thin ledge running above our heads, where you could squeeze another two people if you were desperate. I heard rustling but I was determined to ignore it. Just birds probably. So what? I was too tired to care. Then they moved, scampering from one side to the other. It was impossible not to listen.

'Fucken rats.' Jonathon's water bottle bounced off the boards overhead and I heard the little feet scurrying away. A minute later, just long enough to start to relax, and they were back. Down below our feet this time, where we'd left our packs. I could hear their sharp teeth making short work of our plastic bags. I imagined the diseases dripping off their little tongues and how their scaly tails would feel if they ran over me. I tried to remember whether I'd left anything open. The others definitely had. I'd seen Lisa throwing stuff everywhere, looking for her torch. I waited for someone else to do something. So did the others. Meanwhile the rats got on with their work and the sound of it filled the darkness. I tried to push it aside and lose myself in sleep but every time my thoughts began to break up the sound would start again; another rip, another tear.

A torch came on and I heard the rats disappearing through the cracks and holes. It was Ms Jenkins, sitting up in her sleeping bag, shining the light on to our gear.

'You'll have to check your packs,' she told us. 'If you don't put that food away they'll come back.'

We reluctantly wriggled free from our bags, apart from Rebecca who didn't move.

'All fucken useless,' I heard her mumble. Her pack was just as she'd left it, closed up tight and standing against the wall.

'So who left the bread out?' Jonathon held up the remains of a loaf. In the light of his torch we could see the plastic had been shredded and large chunks of bread were gone. 'Hungry little suckers aren't they? It was your job to pack this away wasn't it Turner?'

'I didn't know you'd taken it out.'

'Should have checked.'

'Anyway, Lisa was carrying it.'

'No, I took the pot remember, after lunch.'

'We stayed here after lunch.'

'For God's sake!' Rebecca sat up, sounding like a babysitter who'd had her favourite movie interrupted. 'One of you just put it away. We'll be dumping it in the morning anyway. Hurry up. I want to sleep.'

'Don't see you helping,' Jonathon said.

'I didn't leave food out, did I?'

'That's right, I forgot. You're perfect.'

'Just less useless than you. There's a big difference.'

'It must be so hard for you.'

'Leave her alone.'

'You fuck up.'

'All of you fuck up and do something with that bread.'

It was just like old times. We packed everything away, exchanged a few more insults and went back to our sleeping bags. The wooden boards felt even harder second time around but still I made it halfway to dreaming before the rats came back. I heard one running along the board that angled down the wall only centimetres above my head. Then it stopped and there was silence, the silence of five people listening for the same sound. Then a second rat making its way down the same board, so close I could smell it, that decaying piss-scent rats have. I pulled my head down into my sleeping bag but it was too hot to breathe.

Something brushed my hair and I froze. Just Rebecca's hand, I told myself. Then Lisa screamed, a sound so sudden and so loud it stayed ringing in my ears, like I was hearing it bouncing its way down the valley.

'My hair! It was in my hair!' She sat up and rubbed frantically at her scalp. 'The little mother was in my hair!'

'Probably got fleas,' Jonathon offered. She hit him hard across the back of his head as he sat up.

'Ow. Just saying.'

'I think one touched my ear,' I told them.

'It's still there!' Lisa screeched. 'Look.'

We followed her torchlight along our sleeping bags. It was perched at the end, close enough that I could reach out and touch it. Its dark eyes regarded us complacently, like it had us well worked out. Jonathon snatched Lisa's torch and hurled it at the little beast. There was a loud crash against the wall, then darkness.

'Now you've smashed the bulb.'

'So you want them to keep coming back do you?'

'They will, now they know what a crap shot you are.'

'Well I can't sleep now,' Lisa announced. 'There's no way I'm even going to try.'

'Lisa.' Rebecca spoke slowly, like she was trying real hard not to lose it. 'Did it bite you? Did it hurt you in any way?'

'No.'

'So ignore it.'

'I can't.'

Ms Jenkins muttered something I couldn't make out, climbed out of her sleeping bag and walked over to her pack.

'Here, I'll light a candle. They won't come back if there's light.' Maybe that was true. Maybe it was Jonathon's torch hurling that had scared them off, or maybe they did return and ran all over my face. I don't know. I was asleep.

When I woke my throat was drier, my head hurt more and I felt like throwing up. Lisa and Jonathon were both making noises that would have terrified me in the dark. Rebecca however was already up, munching her way through a bowl of cereal. We'd gone two nights without decent sleep, we were a day behind schedule, rats had been into our food and the biggest climb lay ahead of us. I got the feeling that in years to come Mr Camden would be using us as his in-class example.

The tramp started with a river crossing which wasn't too bad. It hadn't rained for a while and the water ran clear. From there we dragged our soggy feet up Bull Mound, a two and a half hour slog along a ridge where my moods came and went without warning. We stopped more often than we should have, breaking any rhythm we might have found to drink, blame, and complain. We weren't too unfit as a group. Only Lisa seemed to be really struggling and that was just in bursts. Our weakness was more social.

I was beginning to change my opinion of Ms Jenkins. She didn't seem to have tired at all, even though she'd had as little sleep as the rest of us. She stayed totally even, the same calm mood the whole way. It was like she was quietly letting us know we could rely on her if we had to. I was starting to realise she was the fittest of any of us too. When she walked out front I could see her calves knotting with every step and she never seemed to slip or drop her pace.

The climb was through bush the whole way, beech forest with light undergrowth and the moss getting thicker near the top. The trees thinned out as the ridge flattened to a long spur and we made our way through a new landscape of low scrub and rock. That's when we first heard the wind, roaring across the tops above us. I didn't think much of it, I was too busy trying not to think of sore shoulders or the hours still ahead, or the way I'd walked in on Jonathon and Rebecca talking that morning, and how they'd both stopped as soon as they saw me.

The wind in the Tararuas can only be ignored for so long though. As soon as we came out on to the top of Bull Mound it was obvious this wasn't a place much used to calm. There were no trees up there. The small patches of scrub grew short and prickly, clinging hard to the rocky ground. It was a grey landscape of stone, broken only by vivid green patches of moss. In the background clouds rushed over the tops of the overlooking mountains and then were blown apart, looking like a half-formed waterfall.

We were Wellington kids. We were meant to be used to wind. Down in the city gales funnelled through narrow streets and children grabbed at parking meters to stop themselves blowing away. This wind was different though. This wind was frightening. The noise of it filled my ears as it swept around me, attacking me from three different directions. It inflated my nostrils and twisted my eyelids. It threatened my hold on the ground, 1300 metres up with no place to shelter. Stone cairns pointed the way forward, south along the flat top. At least we would be away from any steep drop-offs.

Instinctively we linked arms. Jonathon paired up with Rebecca while Ms Jenkins and me stood either side of Lisa. We stumbled forward, leaning heavily on one another and crouching to the ground during the strongest gusts. Jonathon was the first to go. They were up ahead of us and I saw him stumble on a rock and lose hold of Rebecca's arm. It was terrifying how quickly the wind took him, lifting his full weight, pack and all, as if he had deliberately leapt into the air. He landed a couple of metres to the left of his take-off point, flat on his pack, arms and legs flailing about like a turtle tipped in the surf.

We got to him as quickly as we could. The wind meant any sound he was making was snatched away before it reached us and it wasn't until I was standing over him that I realised he was laughing. Big whooping laughter, so he had to keep stopping to catch his breath. He grabbed at the arms offered him and pulled himself up.

'Come on,' he shouted in my ear. 'Let's run. That was the coolest thing.'

So we did. The first time the wind took me I freaked, sure I'd land badly, twist a knee or crash head first into a rock. Jonathon was right though, there was fun to be had once I got the hang of it, a bit like moon-walking must feel, only more erratic, taking off in huge wind-assisted bounds, following a crazy path like some Friday night drunk, twisting every time I fell, relying on my pack to cushion me.

Then straight back up and racing to catch the others, our shrieks of laughter ripped away from us, to snag on rocks and branches somewhere down in the valleys. It was a wonderful feeling, to be so totally at the mercy of such an awesome force and yet somehow feel invincible.

At the southern end of Bull Mound a boggy track took us right, down into the shelter of trees. We stopped, the memory of wind still filling our heads, and turned the game into stories. Fifteen minutes on the top had given us enough energy to keep going all the way to Alpha. I remember thinking how once again Jonathon had been the one to pull us together.

The last part of the tramp took us up through the Goblin Forest, where the air is damp all year round and the sky is the only thing not covered by the thick moss. It's a landscape of dripping green, like walking through the set of a movie made for children. We walked in silence, enjoying the tramp now, but ready for the hut too.

It was a huge improvement on Cone, relatively new and built with trampers in mind. A bunkroom overlooked a large open plan kitchen, windows all around let in the light, there was a mattress for every bed and as far as I could tell no holes to let the rats in. Lisa walked over to the map on the wall.

'Look. We did all this today.' She traced the track with her fingers. 'Almost all the climbing done too.'

We crowded round and saw she was right. Alpha Hut was at 1300 metres, not far short of the highest peak for the crossing. We dumped our gear and crashed on the mattresses. There was a sense of relief that we'd beaten the day's challenges. The sort of relief fate lies waiting for.

Dinner was good. It was Rebecca's turn to cook and she produced a huge billy full of curried rice with fresh vegetables and cashews all mixed in. She looked pleased with herself when Jonathon and me raced each other for the seconds. Then we had the predictable washing up argument which I lost, the way I always lose arguments. I run out of volume. After that we did the radio. There was still no acknowledgement from the others who had made it across to Kime before the wind got up. I expected we'd just settle in for a much needed sleep then but Ms Jenkins had other ideas.

'Who's for a walk up to the tops?' she asked us. 'Just fifteen minutes.'

'Walking? Yeah, I knew there was something my day had been missing,' Jonathon replied.

'We'll be seeing it tomorrow anyway won't we?' Lisa asked.

'Not at night we won't. The wind's died right down. It's gorgeous out there.' She rubbed a patch in the steamed up window and the stars shone through. 'You'll be able to see right down into the city.'

'I'm in,' Rebecca announced, sitting up on her bed. She meant it as a challenge and we responded in kind. Even Lisa went through the hell of putting warm feet back into wet socks for the sake of group unity.

The track followed a path waterways had cut through the clay. Soon we were above the trees again and walking through dew-wet clumps of mountain grass. The air was cold and clean-tasting. We all carried torches apart from Lisa but Ms Jenkins made us turn them off, so our eyes could adjust to the light of the low hanging half-moon. She'd been right to drag us out. It was like walking through another world, one where day and night hardly mattered, where none of the things we'd left behind; homework, TV, dodging skateboarders on the pavements, seemed real.

'Now that's a real sky,' Ms Jenkins said, stopping without warning so we all bumped into the person in front. I wasn't prepared for what I saw. The sky was so filled with stars it was more white than black. Their light shimmered, confusing my eyes. I stood there with my head back and my mouth open. It was the sort of night you could drink.

'Fuck that's beautiful,' Lisa whispered to herself, but her voice carried in the clear air and we all murmured our agreement.

From the top we could see the lights of Wellington, down to the south, sparkling around the harbour as if they'd been arranged there especially for our benefit. We found a cavity just off the rim, protected from the breeze, and squeezed in close to one another, for warmth and because we could. Ms Jenkins started the talking. She was beginning to relax with us, now that we were away from the others, away from everything.

She was pointing out the patterns of the stars, explaining to us how to use the Southern Cross to get our bearings, when the first wave hit. I'd been in other earthquakes and at first this one wasn't any different. There's that initial confusion, before you work out for sure what's going on. Maybe it's just some trick of the night, or something wrong with your balance, so you look at the others and see them looking back at you, for just the same reason. Then your senses settle and your brain works out the rest. There's only one thing that can be happening. The ground is pitching and rolling like a ship on an ocean swell, you start thinking about the dangers, all the things that might go wrong. Maybe someone screams or yells out 'cool' and you use it as an excuse to sit even closer. And you wait for it to pass, because it always passes. You ride it out until the ground becomes ground again, a thick crust stretched tight over a liquid earth. Not this time though. This time it didn't stop.

It wound itself up. The rumbling turned to shaking and the shaking turned to waves. It was as if the earth had tired of us and was trying to shake us free. There was noise too, sounds of ground breaking apart and hillsides slipping away, new rips in the earth's fabric. And screaming, my screaming mixed in with theirs, all of us holding tight to each other, like our bodies were the only solid things left. We knew how bad it was without having to say it. At any moment the ground we were perched upon could give way and that would be the end. We would live or we would die and it would all be down to blind luck, nothing else. My mind went numb as I waited, so I felt as if I was watching from the outside. The whole world was breaking free from its rules – even time paused to let the moments fill us, so if you asked how long it lasted, I would have to say forever.

Then it was over, or at least the main shock was, and suddenly only our bodies were shaking. We were all making sounds, strange little noises of fear and relief you won't find in any dictionary.

'The city's gone,' someone finally said. I remember looking to the harbour and seeing only blackness, like the earth had rolled over and turned out the light. There was silence, as we all thought our own thoughts, thoughts of destruction and almost-death. The explosions came in two distinct flashes, each turning to a gigantic fireball rising in the sky, like a fireworks display gone wrong.

'Should we go to the hut?' Rebecca asked, and her uncertainty made it sound like she'd borrowed someone else's voice.

'Not yet,' Ms Jenkins told her. 'There'll be aftershocks. Staying put is the safest thing for now.'

There were three separate waves over the next half hour. The second was the worst, like it was responding to the earlier challenge. It wasn't until we'd had twenty minutes of stillness that Ms Jenkins gave the all clear. No one questioned her authority, or tried to make a joke about this being 'our trip'. We were frightened and we needed her.

She led off slowly, one small step at a time. We had our torches on and walked so close I could feel Lisa's breath on my neck. My legs were unsteady, tight with tramping and fear, and too long sitting in the cold.

'Keep your eyes wide open,' Ms Jenkins instructed. 'Anywhere could be a slip, or a slip about to happen.'

It was too dark to tell how much had changed around us but my imagination filled in the gaps. At one stage the track seemed to finish and we were walking in loose dirt and stones. Then we were squeezing between boulders, too big to have moved surely, but they hadn't been there on the way up.

'Are you sure this is the right way?' Lisa asked from behind me.

'Yeah. Careful up here, it feels quite unsteady. No, come on, it'll be alright.' Ms Jenkins had climbed up over a waist-high boulder. Jonathon followed, then Rebecca. When she reached the top she turned to offer me her hand. Just as I took it the rock moved and she fell forward with a shriek, her weight taking me backwards on to the ground.

'You were supposed to catch me,' she joked, but I could feel she was shaking as much as I was. Below us I heard the huge rock rumbling down the hill before crashing into the scrub.

'Shit.'

'Are you alright?'

'What happened?'

Torches flashed around in the dark. I replied with a weak smile, all I could manage.

It was a relief to see the hut still standing. As far as we could tell the land around it was as we'd left it. Ms Jenkins made us wait outside while she completed three slow circuits with her torch, peering at foundations, kicking at walls and leaning against the water tank. I believed in her, the way you believe in your parents when you're little, because not believing is way too frightening.

When we got inside we just milled around, as if there was something that needed doing but none of us could remember what. I was standing at the bench next to Lisa. She turned and put her arms around me and buried her head in my chest. A candle was lit and the silence broken by the static of the mountain radio.

'This is JG67.' Ms Jenkins was at the table, hunched over the transceiver, talking quietly, no hint of panic in her voice. She was much harder than I would have guessed. 'This is JG67. Do you read me? Over.'

We crowded around her and waited for the static to give way to a reply. Nothing. She tried again, and again. Thirty measured minutes of the same message, like each time she was sure the next one would bring a reply. It never came.

Then we crawled off to our beds, all five of us close together on the bottom level. As soon as my eyes closed my head filled with movement. I fell asleep feeling like a baby again, rocking into unconsciousness.

11.

April 21

I have set myself a target. Three days. In three days the Doctor will be dead. Any longer and I am sure I will be discovered. It seems so simple, when I write it down. The Doctor will be dead. There must be a thousand different ways of killing, in a place like this, and I've had plenty of time to think about it. But the more I think the less simple it seems. Perhaps that is fear.

If nothing else works I will attack him openly, but that must be my last resort. There is a chair in the television room with legs that screw out. One of those in my hand feels good, the right weight to swing. It would just be a matter of coming up behind him, letting go a frenzy of blows to his head, until it is a head no more. I could do that. I could plead insanity easily enough, the Doctor has already made the diagnosis. There would be a price to pay though, a lifetime maybe in a place like this. But I could talk again, and there would be visitors too. It would be worth it. The biggest problems are the possibility of someone intervening, pulling me off before the job was finished, or my strength failing me. I know I couldn't bear that. I couldn't live with another failure.

I have thought of poisoning him. I have even collected all the pills I have pretended to take, hidden them here with my book.

Only I don't know what they are, or how they might affect him, and I have no idea how I would get him to take them. It is not as though he is in the habit of sitting with me as he eats his dinner. And it would happen offstage, his final pain. I don't want that. I want to be there, I want to see it. I want to be part of it.

We are on the third floor here and there is concrete down below. It has become my favourite fantasy, watching him fall through the spaces in between, calling out for help, grabbing desperately for something solid, while his life rushes past and the world looks away. Not that they're stupid enough to leave windows unlocked in a place like this. It wouldn't be long before a flying competition was organised. If only there was a way of luring him out on to one of those balconies. I am thinking I could confront him during his rounds, show him I can talk, lead him there. I have wondered about charging him too, propelling him through the glass. There is a fire escape but I can't see how to get to it. Maybe if I set off the fire alarms there would be a chance. It is still only half of an idea, tied to the picture of the Doctor falling.

I could get someone else to do the job for me. There must be people here who would only need the smallest nudge to get them going, a prod in the psychotic direction. A riot could start, with him in the middle. That would be wild, watching the shit get kicked out of him by a bunch of crazies. Unpredictable though. Risky. Sometimes I wish he was a cat, so he might die nine times over. I would find a way of being there at every one, directing the proceedings.

Or there is the real world. Me here, alone in this little room. It feels colder today. Cold in the air and cold in my bones. The cold of knowing that he must have plans of his own, plotting them right now as I write this down. Three days left and so much work still to be done. I will follow him, next time he comes on the ward. I need more information.

Now I must find words for something else which can no longer be put off. It is the thing that can make sense of all of this, the hardest thing to write.

12.

The next morning I woke slowly. I recognised the pieces of my world but couldn't place them. It was like having a jigsaw shaken loose in front of my eyes. Same hut, same sleeping bag, same faces, but outside a world turned upside-down, and inside my head the memory of the night before. It was hard to know where to start.

At first I concentrated on just being busy, doing all the normal stuff, hoping that would be enough to restore order. We all did. Rebecca got the billy on, Ms Jenkins tried the mountain radio again, Lisa had her morning battle with her gear, swearing loudly at a lone sock and a missing toothbrush. Jonathon sat back and watched, his grin still there but not so certain now, and I opened the stash of gingernuts I had kept for emergencies. I figured this counted. None of us said much.

Ms Jenkins made us all sit down and eat the porridge she had made and while we struggled through it she tried to explain the situation. Her role was clear now. She was in charge and she would get us out safely. The rules had changed.

'Okay then. About today. I went back up on the tops before the sun came up. The lights are still out, right up through the valley too. When it got light, well the damage up here is pretty severe too. There are slips right round the Dress Circle and it looks like a huge crevasse has opened up two thirds around. Below where we were sitting last night a whole spur has basically collapsed.'

'Fuck we were lucky,' Rebecca said.

'It was hard to tell because some cloud has come in now but it looked like there'd been movement off the top of Marchant too. The thing is, I'm no expert but I figure there must be a chance that either of the valleys has been dammed by the slips. What else? The mountain radio is still out which seems strange to me. It means we don't have a forecast so it would be crazy to go over the tops in these conditions I think, especially with so little visibility. I'm thinking that leaves two choices.'

She paused and looked around, like she wanted to make sure we all understood.

'Look, I don't want to get overdramatic here. Rebecca's right, we were very lucky and we're all perfectly safe where we are. The thing is, this is for real now. We have to be careful. Very, very careful. You realise that don't you?'

We nodded. She would be careful, we would do what she told us. It wasn't too difficult.

'Right. Where was I?'

'The choices.' The rest of us were still sitting but Rebecca had finished her food and was standing at Ms Jenkins's shoulder, her self-appointed lieutenant.

'Yeah. Well, we can stay here for another night, maybe even two, and wait for things to sort themselves out down there. The radio will come back on, I'm sure of that, and we can let everybody know we're alright and take advice from the experts. The other option is to very carefully make our way out, back the way we came in. It'll be slow going, depending on the slips, three days maybe, I don't know.'

'Yeah, walk out. Definitely,' Jonathon said.

'Because?' asked Rebecca.

'Food. We stay here and I'm going to starve.'

'There's heaps of food.'

'Not that much.'

'We brought all those emergency rations. We'll be fine.'

'Actually we should sort that out first,' Ms Jenkins said. 'It is a good point. Let's get all our food and bring it here, see what we've got. All of it, secret stashes included.'

What happened next was what I knew would happen. The pile that formed on the table wasn't all that impressive. There was a block of chocolate, a couple of rice risottos, my half-packet of gingernuts, a carrot, a small salami and a packet of squashed bread rolls. Ms Jenkins added cheese, crackers and a huge bag of scroggin but it still looked like our decision was going to be made for us.

'No way.' Lisa looked at the table disbelievingly. 'There was heaps more than that. What about the loaves of bread, and the pasta?'

'Rats got it,' Jonathon reminded her.

'Not the pasta.'

'Yeah, where is it?' Rebecca asked.

I looked at Jonathon and he looked at me and we both thought about lying.

'We, ah, ate it,' I admitted. 'That night at Riversdale, we went out later. We were really hungry, after you burnt the pizza, and ...'

'Who?' Rebecca demanded. 'Who ate it? There were five packets.'

'Me, and Jonathon, and some guys were up playing cards. They helped.'

'It's not like we could have known this was going to happen,' Jonathon tried, but there was no point. It hadn't seemed important at the time, but that was a lame defence and we knew it. Rebecca glared at us both and we stood in embarrassed silence. I hoped Ms Jenkins would come to our rescue but she didn't.

'Maybe there's still enough,' Lisa tried. She looked to Ms Jenkins. 'So what do you think we should do?'

'You tell me.'

'No.' Lisa was adamant. 'You decide. It's too important. We'll just get it wrong.'

'Look, put it this way,' Ms Jenkins said. 'I don't think either option is bad, so long as we're all agreed and sensible. Normally I'd say stay put, no problem, but we don't know how bad things are down in the city. Help might be a while coming. But whatever we decide we all have to do it together, so I want to know what you're all thinking.'

We tried our best to tell her, talking ourselves round in nervous circles. Staying put did seem to be the sensible choice, the sort they'd advise in mountain safety videos. Against that was the fact that we all wanted to get home. The thought of days of just waiting, watching the food pile getting smaller and smaller, worrying about the earthquake, our friends and our families, was too much. We voted three to one in favour of walking out. I was the one. I didn't mean it, I just wanted to show that I could be responsible, after stuffing up with the pasta.

'Let's do it then,' Ms Jenkins said.

'But are you sure it's the right decision?' Lisa pressed.

'Is now. Next thing, go and get your maps and compasses. We need to go over the possible routes out of here.'

'Ah, and if we haven't got maps and compasses?' Jonathon asked. I looked at my feet. So did Lisa. There had been a lunchtime when we were meant to go and pick them up, but the sun had been shining. Another thing that hadn't seemed important at the time.

'Jesus!' Rebecca erupted. 'So you eat our survival rations, you don't have any means of navigation, do you even have raincoats?' I thought guiltily of my jacket, borrowed at the last minute, sort of waterproof.

'Come on Rebecca,' Ms Jenkins said. 'Don't let it get to you.'

'But it does get to me. Look at them. They're all so fucken useless.'

'And you're so perfect,' Lisa replied. That made Jonathon

smile. Me, I didn't much care what she thought. I was tired. Things had screwed up. It was time to go home. In my head the trip was already over. We had failed but it wasn't exactly our fault, that's how I saw it.

Rebecca took her scowl back to her bunk and returned with map and compass. She dropped them on the table in front of us and walked to the other side to share with Ms Jenkins.

'It's a map,' she said. 'It helps if you open it up.'

'Right then.' Ms Jenkins tried to quietly herd us back to more important things. I don't know why she didn't just shout, or slap us about a bit. 'We go back along here, past Hell's Gate. I imagine here, and here, and maybe here too, will be worst hit with the slips. That'd mean big detours. We can't climb above them because it's a ridge so we'll be cutting down through bush a lot. Then, once we get to here, it's either down Bull Mound or along Marchant. Hopefully we'll have a better idea of which will be best by then. You need to make sure your gear is as waterproof as you can make it. I've got spare plastic bags if anyone needs them. I don't know how hard this will be but we should expect to spend at least one night out in the bush. Any questions?'

'Let's just do it.'

'Okay. First though I want to hear how you're all feeling about this. Be honest. Rebecca?'

'I'm okay.'

'Still pissed with the others?'

'A bit.'

'Get over it.' I saw Rebecca thinking about replying but she smiled instead. 'Good. How about you, Jonathon?'

'Looking forward to it.'

'Seriously.'

'Yeah, I'm okay,' he shrugged.

'Lisa?'

'I'm a bit tired I guess, and a bit scared.'

'What of?'

'Not being able to keep up.'

'Right, you walk in the middle then. Okay, we're ready.'

'Ah, Miss.' It was Lisa who noticed.

'What?'

'You haven't asked Marko.'

Ms Jenkins tried to look surprised, and confused too, but I'd seen what had happened. She'd gone blank on my name. Remembered Lisa's, forgotten mine. I was red with embarrassment, and pissed off too. I didn't know I could be so missable.

'So, Marko.' Using my name again, trying to make sure. 'How are you feeling?'

'I just want to get moving,' I replied sulkily, and she left it at that.

'Fair enough. Before you put your packs on I'm just going to have a ten minute run down the track, to make sure it isn't totally impassable. I'll be back soon. Maybe scrub down that bench while you're waiting, eh? And this is the last time you'll be near a long drop for a few days probably. Worth considering.'

She left her pack at the door and was gone. We waited, at first watching Rebecca work on the aluminium benchtop with a disgusting old steelo that had been left at the water tank. Then Jonathon suggested a game of cards but Rebecca said there wasn't time. After that we sat in silence, apart from Lisa asking what the time was and Jonathon saying, 'Told you there was time for a game.'

I didn't think too much of it. I wasn't worried. Ms Jenkins could look after herself. If she was taking her time there'd be a good reason. Only time kept passing.

'She's been gone forty-five minutes now,' Lisa announced. 'It's been too long.'

'There's nothing we can do. She'll be back soon,' Jonathon said.

'But maybe we should go and look for her.'

'Away you go then.'

'I didn't mean me.'

'It's the worst thing we could do anyway,' Rebecca told us. 'You should never split up a group if you don't have to.'

Somehow that really got to me. It was her, talking like she was so much better than us, like we were children. I was sick of it, same as I was sick of being invisible. So I was standing up before I'd even thought about it.

'I'm going out to check anyway,' I said. 'I'll be back in ten minutes.' I was out the door before anyone spoke. I think they were as surprised as I was. No one followed.

Outside the world seemed strangely normal. The bush has a long memory I suppose, it's seen plenty of earthquakes.

There was the familiar smell of damp earth and the leaves were beaded with misty rain. Normal sights. Normal sounds. Darker than I remembered it though, and less friendly. The further I went the more aware I became of the depth of the bush, its shadows. I felt naked without my pack, alone without the others. Although the muddy track was easy to follow I could feel it closing in behind me with every step. I went from a quick walk to a jog, hoping to outrun the fear rising in my throat. I looked for Ms Jenkins around each new bend but there was no sign of her. I wished I hadn't been so quick to prove a point. I wished I was back in the hut with the others. But I kept going.

The first voice I heard was a man's. It was so unexpected it stopped me dead. Although I couldn't make out what he'd said, something in the sound of it kicked at my heart. I looked to where it had come from, past a point where the track curled up over the ridge, out of view. Then came Ms Jenkins's voice. This time I was still and ready, able to make out the words.

'Look, I've already asked you clearly. Please just let me go.' A voice trying to sound calm and reasonable, but breaking up on the sharp edges of panic. That's when I should have acted. I should have shouted out. I should have turned and run back for the others. It wasn't that far. I shouldn't have just stood there, or edged forward the way I did, a stupid, useless spectator.

I crouched as I moved up the track, trying to be silent but finding every twig, every loose stone, with my feet.

'You'll go when we want you to go.'

'You know what this is, don't you? This is assault.'

'This is me not giving a shit actually. We're just being friendly. You haven't even told us your name.'

'Let me go.'

Then I could see them. I was half-lying, leaning into the steps in the track, raising my head up over an exposed tree root. They were only ten metres ahead of me. There are lots of things I have forgotten, but not this. Not a single detail has worked itself free.

There were three men, all with their backs to me. The tallest wore a bright red coat which covered his shorts. His legs were the legs of a tramper, balled calves over thick woollen socks. He had backed Ms Jenkins into a tree and held her wrists above her head, pinned against the trunk. The men on either side were both shorter and wore hooded swandris. One was slender and the other stocky, judging by their legs. The heavier one had a hunting rifle over his shoulder. They both seemed relaxed, as if nothing special was happening. One had his hands stuffed in his pockets, the other's hung loosely at his side.

Most of all I remember Ms Jenkins, or the little I could see of her. She was wearing her dark short-sleeved ice-breaker, and the same grey shorts she'd been wearing the whole trip. I remember one of her bootlaces was undone, and seeing her watch on the ground at her feet. I only caught a glimpse of her face, fighting a battle between anger and control. I felt angry too, and every time I remember it I feel angrier still. Angry at him, at all of them, but angrier at myself. Angry that I didn't move, didn't shout, didn't do a thing. Angry I could be that close, and only stay and watch.

I have tried to tell myself it was because I didn't properly understand what was happening, but that isn't the truth. The truth is, when I was tested, I turned out to be a coward.

'You know something?' It was the tall one who did all the talking. He leaned his weight over Ms Jenkins and my view of her was blocked. 'You're even prettier when you're angry. Do you have a husband back home? Boyfriend?'

'What do you want?'

'I'm sorry. Am I being too subtle for you?'

I don't care what he says. He knew what he was doing. There wasn't any craziness in his voice. It was deliberate, every word of it, every action. Darkly deliberate.

'Fuck you!' That was it. My last chance to act. I've played it out a thousand times since in my head and it is always then, in that split second, when she cracked and there was no more pretending, that I make my move. But there was no move, and my chance was gone.

It all happened so quickly then, unfolding before me like a series of still photographs, flopping one on top of the other, from one horrible image to the next, until the final, inevitable picture comes down. No credits to roll, no names for the actors, no make-up wiped clean or lights coming up.

He lets go of one wrist, moving slowly, confidently, three men and a gun, with no rules to follow, nothing to fear. His hand comes down, brushes her cheek, traces the outline of her breast. She strikes out. Not with her hand but with her knee, catching his groin and doubling him over. She moves forward. I watch. They close in, one on either side, a shoulder each, driving her back against the tree. He recovers enough to stand. An obscenity from him. She returns it. Then the blow, an arm swinging up just as she struggles to get free. Her head is forward when it connects. The impact snaps it back. An awful crack, the back of her skull against the tree. Her body crumples forward. Still I watch.

All three of them, standing over her.

'Jesus, I think you might have …' Silence.

'She's alright. Stand back.'

'No look. There's …'

'Oh fuck.'

'You mean …'

Fumbling about her neck, her head. Then no movement. A stillness and a silence extending through the valleys, emptying me of feeling.

'It wasn't meant to be …'

'You've killed her.'

That simple. That stupid. That small. It isn't meant to be like that. Death should be important. It should be grand. Not just a moment, out of nowhere. Alive, checking out a path, strangers, then, without warning, without fanfare, not alive. It seemed so tiny, so pointless, so ugly.

And as soon as they said it, as soon as I heard the word, I was moving, and they were chasing me.

Even when you're running for your life your body is still

only your body. You don't suddenly sprout wings, or develop superhuman powers, the way they do in the movies. You can't just sprint away at top speed, on and on. Twenty seconds if you're lucky, that's all you get. Then your body is gone. You slow down, you have to. You gasp for air. Your lungs burn, your muscles are emptied, you are reduced to a stagger. New oxygen reaches your legs and you go again, but not sprinting. If the people chasing understand this, they pace themselves. That way, even if they are slower, they will catch you. I was lucky. They were panicking, sprinting too, crashing down the track behind me, giving me a chance. I could hear their footsteps, a desperate rhythm behind me, not gaining, not fading. I hit the wall. My lungs gave out and I was sure they must catch me then but when I looked behind me I saw only the first of them, just in view, but stopped like I was, doubled over, sucking in the air. It gave me hope.

I went again, understanding I would have to settle into a pace I could maintain back to the hut. I am not especially fit but I am seventeen. I don't have a car. I walk places, I play some soccer and am in a touch team. I go to judo twice a week. They were men, years of sitting-down jobs weighing down their legs, years of one-more-round at the pub clinging to their sides. I was getting away from them although I could hear they weren't giving up. I needed to be further ahead, so that when I reached the hut there would be time to warn the others. I kicked again, demanding an impossible effort from my body, looking for another gear. It hurt so much I could taste the vomit in my throat, but then I saw the green roof and my body forgot the pain.

'Guys! Guys! You've got to run!' There was no breath left for shouting and the words barely carried as far as my own ears.

'Hey Marko!' Lisa called out from the balcony, looking too relaxed, not understanding. 'Hey you guys, Marko's back.'

The chasers must have heard and the sound of other voices must have panicked them even more, because a second later a rifle shot exploded into the air, echoing across the scarred valleys. I didn't have to explain.

'Leave the packs, no time,' was all I got out. Alpha Hut has a back door and I ran right through, just hoping they would understand and follow. Later they told me I looked so scared, red and sweating with empty eyes, that even without the gun shot they would have known. I ran hard, up past the long drop, but my legs had gone and they quickly overtook me.

'Where to?'

'The bush,' I croaked. 'Hide.'

We cut back to the right, down off the track, crashing through undergrowth and sliding down steep slopes. After a couple of minutes we stumbled to a stop, pressed in close behind the carcass of a toppled rimu. We waited and we listened, the others with their heads bursting with questions, mine spinning with answers I didn't want to believe.

13.

April 22

Last night he came back round to check on me again. I was awake, waiting. It has got so I can recognise the smell of him now. He is a smoker and doesn't wear aftershave. He carries the scent of freshly washed clothes. I kept my eyes closed and pictured my heart slowing down. I can make that happen now. It is just practice. There was a moment when his breathing slowed too, as if he had realised. The two of us, paused in the darkness, wondering if this might be a good time to kill. Both waiting for the other to make a move. I didn't flinch and neither did he. I heard him walk closer to the end of my bed, where the charts are. He came forward, took my wrist. His fingers were cold against my pulse. He must have felt my heart leap. Then he walked away slowly, his feet barely making any sound against the floor. Only his clicking ankles gave him away. He stopped outside my door for a while, hoping he had tricked me. Or maybe he is becoming afraid. He should be.

I heard him head off down the corridor and moved quickly, slipping out of my bed and across the room. The ward is different at night, a strange place of half-light and half-noises. The gurgles

*and murmurs of tranquillised sleep, crazy people having crazy
dreams, probably not even realising.*

*I walked slowly, hearing everything, the faint tune from a ra-
dio turned down low in the nurses' station, my bare feet breaking
free of the sticky floor. Movement farther down the ward, the
second room from mine, or maybe the third. The Doctor finishing
his rounds, looking in on real patients, patients he doesn't need
to silence. I headed to the visitor's room, thinking I would follow
him when he came back past. I tried to move without making any
sound, wishing I didn't have to spend so long out in the open. I
made the shelter of the dark room and slid behind the half-open
door, listening to my heart slowing down. I crawled to the chair
with the screw-out legs and removed one. My heart sped up with
the feel of it in my hand. I waited.*

*I heard his footsteps approaching and I imagined how he would
look, his tall, unsuspecting strides, his exposed forehead and long
face, empty of guilt. I imagined how it would feel to strike the first
blow and my hand became slippery with perspiration. But the
clicking of his ankles stopped before he reached me. By the sound
of it he was standing outside my room, looking in. I had clumped
the bedclothes into a ridge, so that from the doorway it would
appear I was still sleeping there. Not if he went inside though.
Click. His feet moved forward. A pause, he had noticed, then him
hurrying out again, down the corridor, past me too quickly.*

'Nurse! Nurse!' I heard him whisper urgently.

'What? What is it?' Margaret's voice.

'He's missing. He's not in his bed.'

'Who?'

'Who do you think? The boy.' No need for names or further questions. She understood straight away.

'He might have gone to the toilet,' she whispered. Not 'so what?' Not 'it hardly matters'.

'Why is he awake at all? He should be sleeping all night on fifteen milligrams.'

'You can't always predict ...'

'Don't tell me my job.'

They were edging back towards the nurses' station and their whispers became unintelligible. Not the feel of them though, the urgency, the hint of desperation from the Doctor, telling me that with Margaret he has nothing to hide. And her replies, short, clipped statements, spat out into the corridor like little arrows of warning. I stood there, not daring to move, wondering how much she must have worked out, how much she must have told him. If he knows I have stopped taking the drugs then he must be close to making his move. He must have a plan.

I heard feet moving off towards the toilets. Only one pair I thought, one of them left standing guard. I counted to twenty, willing them to move off too, but there was nothing. I moved out from behind the door and crouching down, my head close to the ground, allowed myself a quick glimpse outside. The Doctor stood with his back to me, watching for Margaret's return. He was five metres away, maybe less, suspicious and alert. A bad time for an attack.

I stood slowly and considered my chances of making it back to my room. The door was almost directly opposite, four paces away, maybe five on the diagonal. I had to try.

I gently balanced on one foot, then the other, rotating the free ankle each time, to make sure they were loose, so they wouldn't creak and give me away. I moved. Quick bounds, landing and pushing off in the same movement, only the balls of my feet touching down. I didn't have the nerve to do it slowly. If he had turned I would have kept moving, down the corridor, back around the other side, away from the ward, away from everything.

He didn't turn though. I made it back to the bed without hearing his voice. The fear had pumped me full of adrenaline and my mind was still racing, looking for a way out, a chance to keep the upper hand. I didn't climb into my bed but instead lay down on the hard floor on the far side, where he might not have looked earlier. I closed my eyes and I waited.

It was ten minutes before they returned, both of them together, still talking in broken, impatient whispers.

'You see, I told you. He's gone.'

'No wait, look over here.' Margaret's footsteps came around to my side of the bed. 'Here he is, look. He's climbed down onto the floor, silly thing.'

There was a long pause, the Doctor looking closely, making up his mind about what he was seeing.

'Has he done this before?'

'I don't know.'

'Get him back into bed then.' Still angry. Still uncertain.

Margaret shook me and I let myself seem half-awake, groggy and confused. I saw the Doctor had already left. Margaret didn't say a word as I climbed back into my bed.

Now I'm hurrying to get this down, writing so quickly I can

barely recognise my words. It is the last thing I know, the only
thing I am still sure of. Time is running out.

14.

We heard them crashing about in their search, calling out
to one another. They had lost track of us and there was no
system to their hunting but that didn't make me any less
afraid. We kept our heads down and stayed silent. I listened
to the men regrouping on the track above us. They were
arguing about something. The voice I recognised rose higher
than the others, shouting them down. Then we heard them
moving back towards the hut.

'Jesus Marko, what was all that about?' Jonathon asked,
and I could tell by his voice he wasn't close to getting it. He
was expecting a story, a full stop at the end, something we'd
look back on and laugh about. Not what I had to tell him at
all, which was just a beginning, with us right in the middle
of it. I didn't want to speak. I wanted to be anywhere else
but there. I wanted there to be some way of them knowing
without me having to say it.

'Come on Marko, you're scaring us,' Rebecca said.

'It's Ms Jenkins isn't it?' Lisa guessed.

I nodded and opened my mouth, determined to form the words. Any way would do. There was no right way. Everything about it could only be wrong.

'I saw them. They killed her. She's dead. Ms Jenkins is ...'

That was all I could do. I heard my own words and choked on the sound of them. I didn't cry, I just stopped. Stopped talking, stopped feeling. There was emptiness all around me, on their faces, in the air, sucking us dry. We didn't speak, we didn't move, we couldn't even look at one another. None of us knew what came next.

'God.' From Lisa. Not a word, more a whimper.

'You wouldn't joke about this would you?' Jonathon asked, but his voice was too quiet, too soft to be his. 'No, you wouldn't. Sorry. Shit.'

'You sure?' Rebecca asked. I nodded. 'Well, how? What happened?'

It had to be asked and it had to be told. They gathered behind her question and I explained to them what I had seen, every awful detail of it. When I finished they looked confused, like I'd missed out some crucial point, the thing that would make sense of it all.

'But who are they?' Lisa asked.

'I don't know. You saw as much of them as I did.'

'Not really.'

'Just people. People who are fucked up. I don't know.'

'But why had they stopped her? What did they want?'

Lisa wouldn't let herself understand.

'What do you think?' Rebecca replied, her voice so drained it sounded heartless.

'No. No, that can't be right. Nobody ... not three of them. Not tramping. It doesn't happen like that. People wouldn't.'

'They did.'

'No, you must have got it wrong Marko. You must have misheard them. Or something else must have happened, before you got there.'

I knew what she was getting at. The same thing I wanted, some way of making it all not so bad, better somehow. Only there're some things that can never be made better. It could have been a total accident. It could have happened while they were trying to help her. She'd still be dead. All the things that were Ms Jenkins, they'd still all have stopped. She wouldn't laugh now, or complain, sweat or even breathe. Never. So how can that be made any better?

'But what exactly killed her?' Rebecca asked me. 'You don't just kill someone with a punch.'

'It was her head I think, against the tree.'

'But you're sure she's dead?'

'They checked. They said she was.'

'She might not be then,' Lisa decided.

'She is, okay Lisa?' Jonathon snapped. 'She is.'

'Who?' Lisa asked. I thought she'd lost it completely then.

'Ms Jenkins,' I replied, as gently as I could, scared she would scream, give our position away.

'No, I mean her name. What's her name? We should be

using her name.'

But none of us knew her name. For me that was one horrible thought too many. The pain started in waves behind my forehead and washed out as tears, loosening every muscle, wasting every expression, until the sobbing was uncontrollable.

'Hey, it's okay Marko,' someone said, only it wasn't, so soon they were crying too.

We couldn't stay like that forever. We needed a plan, but without Ms Jenkins there was no one to suggest it. In the end it was Rebecca who was strongest.

'We can't stay here,' she told us. 'We have to get back to the hut.' She wasn't ordering us around, she was just being our example. 'We have to get our gear.'

'Then what?' Lisa asked.

'We walk out of here, tell the police. First though we should go back to where she died, see if we can tell what they've done with her.' Rebecca was back to being Rebecca now, speaking with quiet certainty.

'Sounds dangerous,' Jonathon said.

'We owe it to her.'

'They might be waiting for us in the hut,' I pointed out.

'No, they'll have panicked. They'll be wanting to get as far away as they can, cover their traces.'

'I'm their traces,' I reminded her.

'He's got a point,' Jonathon agreed.

'So what are you saying we should do?' Rebecca snapped at him. The old tension, but with new reasons now.

'I'm saying we should be careful, that's all,' Jonathon said, backing down from the fight.

And we were careful. We spent half an hour creeping the 500 metres back to the hut, and another half hour after that circling round, looking for signs of life. Jonathon volunteered to go inside first. He was meant to give a morepork call once he'd decided it was safe, a bit useless in the daytime but it was the only one we could think of. It didn't matter anyway, because what he called out instead was 'Fuck them!' loud and angry. We were still trying to work out whether that counted as an all-clear when he appeared on the balcony.

'Are you coming in or what?' he called to us.

'We didn't hear your morepork,' Rebecca told him.

'The morepork says "fuck them". Come and look at what they've done.'

They'd been through all our packs, taking the food, the sleeping bags and most of the clothes. What little was left was strewn about the floor.

'Now we're screwed,' I said, even though I knew it didn't help to say it. Nobody disagreed.

I think when you're faced with something like that, a situation so serious it could kill you, there's a battle that goes on between two parts of your brain. There's one part that always wants to keep on fighting, no matter how impossible everything seems. Then there's another part that's always only the smallest excuse away from giving up. I think those parts are always there, and most of the time we never find out which is strongest. For us, over the next ten minutes, in amongst the mess of our few discarded possessions, our heads full of shock, the giving-up parts started winning. We sat around and started talking and all any of us could say was how terrible it had all become.

Then something else started happening, with Jonathon and Rebecca. Whatever one of them said, the other one attacked, like there was a battle for control going on. Jonathon wanted to stay put in the hut. He said it was too dangerous to go out without any gear, and it would be the first place Search and Rescue would come looking, when they realised we were missing. More though, I think it was just because Rebecca still wanted to move on.

'You can't rely on Search and Rescue,' she said. 'If there still is a Search and Rescue they'll be too busy digging people out from buildings. The only people coming back here are those bastards and their guns.'

'You've changed your tune.'

'I've had time to think about it.'

'Well you were right first time. They will have freaked. Think how you'd feel if you'd accidentally killed someone.'

'It wasn't an accident.' She sounded so sure, for someone who hadn't been there. 'They're murderers.'

'So you seriously think we can walk out of here, without getting lost, or starving, or freezing to death?' Jonathon challenged.

'Yes.'

'Away you go then.'

'You're all coming with me.'

'Pass.'

'You don't speak for the others.'

I didn't want to have to decide, same as I didn't want them to argue. I wanted there to be just one option, and I wanted someone to explain it to me. Rebecca did her best.

'We won't get lost. We head east, into the morning sun. Two valleys and we're out of here. What did it take to walk in here? Not much, right? And this time there's no gear to carry. It's two days max. We won't starve. You can go weeks without food, if you have to. All we need is water and there isn't exactly a shortage of that up here. And freezing isn't going to be a problem either. Look, they've left the packliners. Jonathon, pass that stupid knife you're always carrying.'

'What are you going to do, Xena, hunt us some dinner?'

'Just do it.' Rebecca flipped open the blade and with three neat slits the bag became a raincoat. 'So we go. Come on you two, what do you say?'

I wanted to believe her, because it was so much better than believing nothing. And I knew staying in the hut frightened me more than the bush did.

'Yeah, it does make more sense,' I said.

'I think so too,' Lisa agreed, but she sounded even less convinced. Jonathon looked at me like I'd personally betrayed him.

'Don't say I didn't warn you,' he muttered.

'So it's agreed then?' Rebecca stared straight at him, forcing him to concede.

'You're the boss,' he shrugged.

'Good. Right then, let's get everything together that might be useful and stuff it into this spare packliner. We'll put it in Lisa's pack, it's the smallest. Marko, can you take us back to where it happened?'

'What do we want to do that for?' Jonathon challenged. 'I thought we were in a hurry to get out of here.'

'I want to find her body.'

'Don't see why. She'll still be dead.' I don't think he thought about how that was going to sound. If he didn't realise as soon as he said it, it came to him a second later in the form of Rebecca's fist. Not a 'stop pissing me off' warning blow but a full blooded punch that knocked him off his feet. When he stood back up his nose was bleeding.

'What the fuck was that for?' Jonathon asked, not just to Rebecca but to all three of us, standing in a line now.

'No jokes about her okay?' Rebecca said.

'She's right,' Lisa added. 'We have to find her body. For the family.'

'And it will be evidence,' I added. That came out badly.

'Okay, whatever. I'm sorry. Lead on then, mighty one.'

As we packed together the few warm clothes we had, along with an extra stash of scroggin Jonathon had hidden in a sock, the air was tense. Tense with Jonathon and Rebecca, but more tense with Ms Jenkins, who was already getting difficult to mention.

I led them back to the place, not letting myself feel anything, preferring the numbness of the watching bush, bush that could outlast blizzards or earthquakes, floods or fires, and could keep on coming back. Twice we stopped because someone thought they'd heard something but both times were false alarms. When we finally reached the rise in the track I had to walk back round the corner to be sure. It looked so unremarkable, so like everywhere else, as if nothing unusual could have happened here. Nothing important.

But it was the place and it was the tree. Jonathon got on his hands and knees and found a stone with dried blood on it. He held it out on the palm of his hand and we all looked but nobody touched it or said a word. He let it drop back to the ground. It became impossible to keep out the memories. Ms Jenkins, so far away from dying, just pissed off and tired and not needing their aggro. Death, with no sense of occasion, turning up anyway, uninvited.

'They've hidden her somewhere,' Rebecca said, sounding less sure of herself now we were there. 'Somewhere easy. They will have been panicking. Any ideas?'

'Bush is thickest down that way,' I said.

'Other side's off the track though,' Lisa noted.

'There's a slip over there.' Jonathon pointed ahead. 'That's where I'd put her. Easy to dig up later, and it could look like she died in it.'

'We'll split up then,' Rebecca said. 'Yell out if, well, you know.'

'I'm not going by myself,' Lisa told her. 'I'm going with you.'

We looked. I scrambled down the nearest slope, knowing how important it was to find her, but hoping we wouldn't too. I didn't know how I would handle it. I was already close to breaking up. The shout came from Rebecca, on the other side of the ridge. I met Jonathon on the way back up. He caught my eye and raised an eyebrow. I shrugged. I saw his shoulders rise as he took a deep breath, preparing himself.

I suppose it should have been easiest for me. I'd already seen her. I was there when it happened. Still, I was the first one to turn for the support of a tree, and then, sinking to my knees, throw up. I looked back to the others, still standing over her, looking down like their eyes couldn't turn away until their brains properly understood. Only that would take forever.

She'd been moved quickly, dragged, by the amount of dirt on her clothes, then dropped into a cavity beneath the roots of a fallen tree. A single punga frond was draped over her. It was a careless, hurried attempt at hiding her. On the side of her forehead congealed blood had stuck down a clump of hair.

'Fuck,' Jonathon groaned, low and toneless. It was Rebecca who stepped closer and put her arm around him. I still hadn't been able to get to my feet. Lisa stood alone.

'We should move her,' Lisa said. 'Take her someplace so they can't find her. In case they come back. We could bury her and mark it out, for later. For the police.'

No one disagreed.

'Where?' Rebecca asked.

'How about Jonathon's idea? Down at the bottom of the slip.'

'It'd be easy to find later.'

'Okay.'

Then we waited, like we were hoping something else would happen, so we wouldn't have to do this thing. Nothing did, so we waited some more, for the strength we needed. Then, cautiously, we moved. We started out trying to be gentle, like you might imagine an undertaker would do it, quiet and dignified. But this was the outdoors, steep and awkward. This was a different sort of death. It was real. The body was heavy and we were tired. We took a limb each, although that meant her head hung back, the way you'd never want to see it. I didn't want to look, or smell, or hear. I didn't want any of those things getting inside my head because I knew they'd never get out.

Halfway up the slope I let go. I staggered to the side and retched again but my stomach was empty. I was shivering with cold, my head was fuzzy and my legs collapsed beneath me. I felt the dampness of decaying leaves against one cheek, while tears ran down the other. It wasn't happening. None of it was happening.

'Hey Marko.' It was Lisa, hand on my shoulder, speaking softly, not letting me get away. 'It's okay.'

'I'm sorry,' I spluttered. 'I can't. I just can't.'

'It's alright. We'll manage.'

So I stayed there, I don't know how long, hugging my knees to my chest, thinking nothing, being nothing, while the others got on with doing what had to be done. I was useless. When it really came down to it, when we all had to be strong together, I was useless. I let them down, Ms Jenkins too.

When I walked back to the ridge and looked down, they'd already clawed a shallow grave in the loose dirt of the slip. By the time I got down there they were covering her over. No one spoke to me as I tried to help, losing myself in the feel of the soil in my hands.

'We should say something,' Lisa said, when we'd finished.

'Like what?'

'I don't know. Something about her.' I tried to think but I knew no words would come. Then a gun shot exploded above us. I looked up to see all three of them standing together on the track, less than a hundred metres above us. Ms Jenkins might have been an accident. The next one wouldn't be.

We ran, down through the thick bush below the slip, Rebecca leading, Lisa's light pack slung over one shoulder and bouncing wildly, as if it was as frightened as the rest of us. Below me I could hear the chatter of a stream, mixed with the heavy breathing of the others. Above me I could hear the men giving chase.

15.

April 23
This is all I have left, a makeshift rope, plaited together from the strands of my ripped up pillowcase. Just one thing. Enough to strangle him. He has made his move. In this game of nerves he has called my bluff and I have been forced to take a risk. Now I have one chance left, that is all.

The nurse came early this morning, just after changeover, when the ward is still dark and ruffled by the sounds of bad sleepers. I hadn't seen her before. I woke as soon as the sound of her approaching feet reached me. It is almost three weeks since I slept properly. I could tell from the way she hurried into the room she wouldn't be the type to bother much with small talk or smiles. Head down, one job at a time, trying not to look at the clock, trying to think of the car she's only half paid for, or the next rostered weekend off. I must have been her first task for the morning and she was too busy getting into the routine of it to notice me much. Too busy to see my eyes widen with fear or the sweat of panic breaking over my forehead.

She'd wheeled in a metal stand, an IV bag already hooked in place on the gleaming upright frame. She had the needle out of its sterile bag and held it up in a gloved hand. The Doctor's instructions of course. My stunt the other night hadn't fooled him.

Maybe he has known all along. I couldn't know what was in the bag and I couldn't ask. I could guess though. A nightmare of possibilities scratched at my eyes and expanded in my throat. I wanted to resist. I wanted to thrash about. I wanted to scream out 'no!'. I wondered how long it would take before the will to escape was drowned. I looked at the nurse again. What would she do if I fled? Would she be the type to raise the alarm quickly, or give chase herself? Yes, she would hunt me down, I was sure of it. It was her job, her car, her winter holiday.

A teacher once told me the most important decisions in life have the knack of not seeming all that important at the time. Not this one. It was life and death. That simple, that obvious, that important. And I only had a second to decide. Inside my head I flipped a coin and watched it tumble. I would wait it out. A huge risk, but my best chance.

I tried to swallow the panic. She took my hand. Hers felt cold, mine must have been burning up. She didn't seem to notice. She swabbed the vein on the back of my hand and with a minimum of fuss, as if it meant nothing at all, slipped in the first needle. Just a saline flush but still I winced at the cool of it, clearing a path for the executioner. I told myself it would be slow-working, if it was a drip. A desperate hope, nothing more. I began to count. Two minutes. I would give it two minutes. One hundred and twenty quietly ordered seconds to get through, no more. I made that promise to myself. Surviving is all about keeping promises. The second needle. She checked the bag and let a drip run free. A drip of what? She connected the tube and the count began.

My mind played tricks, feeling heavy, feeling fuzzy, paralysed by fear and imagination. The nurse took her time cleaning up, as if her next job was one she fancied even less. I felt my foot begin to shake. I tensed my whole leg until it felt as if it might snap, hoping she wouldn't notice. I counted.

At seventy-five she checked the drip line. I closed my eyes. At eighty-five she had turned away. She was leaving. On ninety-five I sat up and ripped the needle free, tearing away the transparent tape on my hand. Still I counted, like the number line stretching out ahead of me was a path I could follow, all the way to sanity.

They had taken all my clothes but old Mr Smythe in the bed next door was allowed his RSA blazer. I walked around his bed to where it was draped over the back of his chair, smelling of hair oil and dandruff and a life lived past the point of caring. I am past that point too now. Way past. I put the jacket on and returned to my bed for the pillowcase.

I could have walked out then, left here for good, defeated but alive, but that can not happen. It is another promise I have made to myself. I can not go on that way, failing every time it matters.

The nurse had done me a favour, coming so early. The ward was dark and quiet and slipping out was easy. I made straight for the boiler room, a place to sit and think and work out what happened next, what things had changed. That was the hardest time, sitting there, knowing how easy it would be to walk out, back to all the things, all the people I can't bear to let myself think about. I only had to let their faces into my mind – Mum, Duncan, the others – and my determination would have dissolved. I started to play games inside my head, justifying my weaknesses, imagining outcomes that could never be real.

I imagined going to the police and telling them my whole story. In my version they listened and took notes and I led them to the Doctor, and he screamed out for forgiveness as they led him away. Then I got real, thought how I would look to them, an escaped psychiatric patient, with every single worker on the ward happy to verify my condition. And the Doctor, who isn't stupid, and has had plenty of time to cover his tracks. He'll have a careful answer ready for every question that might be asked. And I'm the only witness, the only one who saw his face. Even if I did get lucky, even if I found someone prepared to push their doubts aside, and the Doctor has been careless, then what? Months of trials, questions and doubts, and appeals and stupid juries, like the ones you hear about all the time, too scared to be certain of anything. Ending where? A comfortable sentence in a comfortable prison, halved for good behaviour.

So even in my weakest moment, alone in that cold room, just this book for company, I knew I had to keep the promise. For Ms Jenkins, for the others, for me. Just this once I have to get something right, something important. I have to stay here. I have to hunt him down, the way he hunted us. I had just decided this, put my mind to planning out the next move, when the door swung open.

I leapt to my feet, knocking the chair to the floor, filling the room with the sound of my panic.

'Jumpy aren't we?' Andrew smiled, edging into the room, watching me carefully like he half-expected me to jump him. Then he gently closed the door.

'So, you talking yet?' he asked, casual, as if he was asking about the weather. He picked up the chair and sat down on it himself, so I was standing over him. I like Andrew, even though I was trying hard then not to. He doesn't rush things, he eases into them. There's a calm surrounding him, a tempting place, where you could pull in for shelter.

'Everyone's looking for you, you know. They've called the police. There are fears you might be dangerous, without your medication. What do you think of that?'

I thought many things but I kept them to myself.

'You can't stay here you know. They'll find you for sure. The maintenance people are in here every second day. They're due this afternoon. So if you're thinking of running, now would be the time to go.'

I listened hard, trying to hear the things he wasn't saying, like what he was doing here, and why he was so sure I could understand him. I kept returning his stare, buying myself time. I could attack him or I could trust him. They were the only options and I wasn't ready to decide.

'What was it that spooked you anyway?'

I stayed silent.

'I heard they were putting a line in, that you were showing signs of dehydration. Water's not so much to be scared of. Did you think it was something else?' He leaned forward, as if expecting me to whisper an answer.

'So what's it going to take to get you talking?'

More information, I wanted to say. Some way of knowing I can trust you.

'I'm not going to make you go back you know, not if you don't want to.'

Then I spoke. Not because I wanted to, not because I had decided I should trust him, but because I had run out of options.

'I need you to hide me.' The words caught in my throat, like a car coughing to life on a cold morning. Still, he understood me well enough. His eyes brightened and his smile changed shape.

'And why should I do that?' he asked. I didn't answer. 'Come on. Who are you? What's your story? I'm curious, nothing else. Tell me and I'll help you. That can be our deal.'

I shook my head. That price was too high.

'Do you even know where you are?'

'Of course.' This time my voice felt more my own. 'Hospital. Palmerston North.'

'Well done. Ward 10 actually.' He leaned forward, like he was about to share some secret. 'It had been closed, lack of funding, you know, but then after the earthquake they needed more emergency facilities. Only, the lifts are out, so they moved psych over here and they're using that now. The thing is they're so desperate for beds now they're pushing most people out as soon as they can. Not you though. Why not? Have you even had any visitors? I haven't seen any. Were you in the city, when it happened?'

I shook my head. 'Just hide me.'

'Why?'

'You don't need to know.'

'Then I can't help.'

It was too much. Now that I was talking again keeping anything else reined in was so hard. My rage snapped loose. I hauled him out of the chair and drove him back against the concrete wall. He was light and barely resisted. The anger inside me made me strong, strong enough to destroy him, if I had to. I held him there and tried to clear my mind.

'I can't tell you anything but I do need your help.' I spoke slowly, like the words could carry more weight, falling one at a time. 'I need a place where no one will look for me. Just for one night. That's all. Please.'

I let him go but I didn't step back. I waited for his reply. He breathed slowly out, stepping forward so his breath mixed with mine.

'You're a strange one,' he finally said, 'and I've seen a few.' Then, 'alright, follow me.'

No more deals, no more questions, just giving in, or helping out, leading me to this new place, where I'm sitting now. It's another small room, this time in the half-completed new wing where, according to Andrew, a bankrupt construction company saw the project stall. The walls are unfinished cladding board and there's even a cavity behind one, where I can hide if I hear anyone coming. The power is on which is lucky, the room has no windows. Andrew left half an hour ago. He promised to come back later, with some food and drink. I think this is like an adventure to him, a welcome change from mops and bedpans. I just hope he isn't obvious about it.

I am beginning to feel optimistic again. For the first time since I came here the Doctor has lost sight of me. That must worry him, it must give me the upper hand. Tonight I will slip out and properly get my bearings. I will find a place to sit and watch. If the Doctor is on duty tonight, he is dead.

16.

When you're being chased the only thing you want to do is keep running, but in the bush that's stupid. As we careered downwards the ground became steeper, vines threatened to snare us, tree roots and loose stones made plays for our legs. It was easier for the hunters. They were less panicked, and this time it sounded as if they had learnt to pace themselves, following the sounds of our crashing. They would have caught us for sure, if Rebecca hadn't decided to stop running and hide. With the darkness of the undergrowth and the land falling away in so many different directions, there was a good chance they wouldn't find us.

She stopped suddenly and turned with a finger to her lips, then cut to the side, where a tangle of moss and creepers covered an uneven landscape of rocks and rotting trees. She found a hollow and ripped back the leafy covering. Then she was gone. We followed her as quickly as we could, Jonathon, Lisa, then me. Being at the back I could imagine what a tempting target I would make from above and waited for the sudden fiery pain of a bullet. But we had a good enough lead on them and I squeezed my way into the makeshift cave while our hunters were still battling with the bush high above us. It was an excellent hiding place, for two people. Four was definitely pushing it. We were squashed so tight I could feel other heartbeats vibrating through my body. I knew part of my back was still exposed but there was no way forward. The air quickly became hot and tasted of dirt and decay. I felt a beetle scratch its way across my head but I couldn't move.

They were still running when they came past us, spread out now, going by the footsteps. It was a minute more before they realised.

'Which way?' someone shouted from below. 'Are they in your direction?'

'Don't think so. Keep going down maybe.'

'Nah, the little bastards have gone to ground. Look around.'

'Should have brought Porker with me. Sniff 'em out no worries.'

'Okay, shut up. We're not going to hear them with you two going on.' That was our cue to all breathe in at the same time. I felt the pressure around me increase. Suddenly I wanted to giggle, like it was some backyard game of hide'n'seek. Someone else was shaking, probably Jonathon. They were trying to kill us and we were fighting back the urge to jump out shouting, 'ha, fooled ya!' I was never made to be a hero.

They spread out and moved slowly back up the slope. With only three of them there wasn't much chance of their covering the area properly. I heard them kicking at ground and breaking back branches, hoping to get lucky. One of them almost did. His foot came down so close to my nose I could smell it. I felt Lisa squeeze my hand. I didn't know she'd been holding it. I squeezed back and the foot moved on, distracted by some other shadow. We heard them move away. Then I felt Jonathon struggling to get up.

'Not yet,' Rebecca whispered.

'I've got fucken cramp,' he replied.

'So rub it.'

'Jesus.' But he settled back down.

'So when can we go?' Lisa asked.

'When it's dark.'

That took another two hours, split into regular intervals by the indiglow on Lisa's watch. By then I'd cramped up too and standing was painful. Straight away Jonathon was off, heading further down the slope.

'Where are you going?' Rebecca demanded.

'Taking a crap, Mummy, if that's alright. Don't suppose any of you brought toilet paper.'

'Sorry, left it with my hair dryer.'

'Leaves it is, then.' And he was gone.

'Ah, actually ...' Lisa said.

'Same,' Rebecca grinned. We all headed off in carefully opposite directions, but none off us went too far, judging by the sound of the crashing about. There were worse things than lack of privacy just then. As bonding experiences go it was probably one of the tackier ones but somehow it worked.

'Shiny leaves or prickly?' Jonathon asked when I returned, last back. It was good to be able to smile.

'So what's the plan?' I asked.

'I think they'd kill us if they could,' Rebecca said. 'We have to be so careful.'

'Do you think they've found Ms Jenkins?'

'Dunno.'

'We still do what we planned,' Rebecca told us. 'Straight out and tell the police.'

'Yeah,' Jonathon agreed. 'So first we find a place to sleep. I'd advise against that little pile of rocks down by the fallen log.'

'No, we move now,' Rebecca corrected, just when I thought their arguments might be over.

'What?'

'If we walk at night and sleep during the day there's no chance of them seeing us.'

'There's no chance of us getting out more like. What about the slips? What about not having a compass? And we're all knackered. Bad move Rebecca. Very bad move.'

'Do I have to hit you again?'

'I'll be ready this time.'

Rebecca turned to me and Lisa. Even in the darkness I could tell how tired she was and I felt sorry for her.

'Come on you two. There's a moon. It won't be that bad. Don't think about being comfortable, think about being alive.'

'Yeah, I'm with you,' I said.

'You're going soft,' Jonathon told me and he sounded properly bitter.

'Lisa?'

'Yeah, okay, but we have to stay close together. And heaps of stops.'

'Right.' Rebecca picked up the pack. 'I think we should stay down at this level, head straight along, then up onto the ridge past Hell's Gate. Over there there's another track, down off Marchant. It's not maintained any more but I've been down it once with Dad. It'll take us to the river. We can camp there, this side, away from the track. It'll be slow, at night and with the slips, but we should make it.'

'And if the river has dammed up?' Jonathon asked.

'Then it has.'

Tramping at night is slow and dangerous. Tramping at night with no torches, no map, no compass, with no track to follow and the whole place split apart by an earthquake, goes way beyond that. Fear kept us close, tripping over one another the whole time. With my arms held out in front of me, to fend off branches I couldn't see, I found my balance went. I shuffled more than walked, feeling the ground ahead of me, going incredibly slowly but still keeping up. I don't know how Rebecca, who stayed at the front, kept her bearings. To me it felt like we were zig-zagging about, until I couldn't even be sure which way was up. We walked straight over the first slip. We didn't even realise until we were halfway across. It wasn't the first bank we'd slid down but when we walked our feet sank and loose dirt ran over our boots like sand.

'This is a slip isn't it?' Lisa asked, her voice full of fear.

'Which makes this fucken stupid doesn't it?' Jonathon asked when Rebecca didn't reply. Again there was no response, she just kept moving forward and we kept following her. I wondered if maybe Jonathon had been right. Maybe this was the wrong call.

'What's the time?' Rebecca asked at our first stop, when the ground seemed to have finally flattened out. We'd been past one more major slip, this time climbing over it. It felt like I'd been stepping through the darkness forever, a million numb seconds.

'Ah, half-past one.'

'So we've been going for what, about six hours? Another four at least before it's light. I think this is Marchant and the ridge we want is through there.' Probably she pointed. I didn't bother pretending to look. I knew she was just guessing. I hoped she was good at it. 'We'll make the river tonight then it's just one more night's tramp and we're out of here. How are you all feeling?'

'You want the truth?' Lisa asked.

'Edit.'

'I'm shaky. I think I might faint soon.'

'I'm fucken thirsty,' Jonathon said.

'Marko?'

'My head hurts, I'm sort of hungry but I also feel like throwing up, my feet are sore, just the usual.'

'But you can do the next bit right?'

I thought about how badly I just wanted to drop to the ground and sleep, but that wasn't what she was asking. 'Yeah, I'm up for it.'

'Okay then.' Jonathon blew the words through his lips. I don't think he wanted Rebecca's job of leading any more.

'Onward,' Lisa said, trying to sound up about it. 'But if I fall asleep and my legs keep moving, don't any of you bastards go waking me.'

I don't much understand people like Mr Camden, who go tramping just for the fun of it. I've always thought a slog uphill should lead to some reward, like the downhill blast you get with mountain biking. With tramping though, going downhill just brings a different sort of pain. Although Rebecca was sure we were following a track, the terrain we stumbled down was steeper than any track I've ever seen. At first we took it slowly, trying to remain upright most of the time, but soon gravity took over. That's when it started to feel unreal, when all the struggling to stay awake, the worrying and the hunger, collapsed. We were sliding on our arses, grabbing at roots or branches for steering, navigating off the sounds of each others' laughter, wrapping ourselves round the shaky thin punga trunks when we needed to stop, or aiming at someone else and hoping they were firmly anchored. It was like being in the wind up on Bull Mound again, danger turned to fun for a moment, ignoring loosened rocks and sheer drop-offs and slips we couldn't see. Not even worrying how our voices might carry. I was past caring. I only had energy left for movement, and for fun.

Only it wasn't like that for Rebecca. Rebecca still had to lead, she still had to worry about where we were headed. It's amazing we went so long without an accident. That's how hard Rebecca is. We were close together when it happened, close enough to see her disappear over an edge that had come up too quickly in the darkness, with just enough time to stop ourselves from following. It wasn't a sheer drop, but steep enough for her to lose control. We heard her crashing down through the bush and we heard her swearing too. Then silence, and one last 'fuck' from somewhere below.

'You alright?' Jonathon shouted but there was no answer.

Lisa led the way, cutting to the left until the way down became flatter. We called Rebecca's name as we walked back around.

'Yeah, over here,' she finally responded, when we were almost on top of her. She was sitting up, Lisa's pack still on her, her head dropped down between her knees. We stood around, feeling useless.

'You okay?' I asked. That was as far as my first aid skills went. She lifted her head and looked at me. I couldn't see her face properly but I could imagine the exhaustion painted there.

'I'm just so fucken tired, you know?' she whispered. Lisa sat down and put her arm around Rebecca's shoulders.

'You're fucken amazing, actually,' Lisa told her. I moved behind them and sat down close on the other side.

'Gee, I feel left out now,' Jonathon mocked.

'Plenty of room.'

'She's right.' He stood back and from somewhere produced a cigarette and a lighter. We sat in silence and watched the glowing tip, brightening and fading with every breath. When it was finished he flicked the stub to the ground and I started, like I'd been half-dozing in front of a television and the screen had gone suddenly blank.

'We could just camp here tonight, if you want,' Jonathon said.

'Nah,' Rebecca shook her head. 'We have to get to the water. The river's close now. I can hear it.'

I listened but couldn't make it out, just the wind in the trees.

'Do you want someone else to lead for a while?' Lisa asked.

'No, I'm just being soft. Come on.' She stood up and we did the same.

'Give us a sec eh?' Jonathon asked. He took two steps to the nearest tree, supported himself with one hand against the trunk, and threw up. None of us asked how he was when he'd finished. Shocked, exhausted, past tired, past hungry, we all knew. If there'd been anything left in my stomach I would have joined him.

It took another two hours to reach the water, most of that spent back-tracking when we encountered a drop-off which was impassable. The path the waterway had cut through the bush was flooded with moonlight. It was like walking into the middle of a day after the near blackness of the bush. We looked around one another, all of us trying to pass off our exhaustion with a grin, no one ready to mention the next disappointment. The water we'd found wasn't much more than a stream. It definitely wasn't the Tauherenikau. We were lost.

'I'm sorry guys,' Rebecca said, not needing to explain.

'Doesn't matter.' It didn't. We were too tired for things to matter.

'Let's just drink and find a place to crash then.'

I gulped down as much as I could from my cupped hands. The water felt heavy in my stomach but couldn't fill it in the way food would have. I tried not to think about how hungry I was becoming.

We quickly found a spot that would do for sleeping, a small area only a few metres square but flat at least, covered in clumps of cutting grass. Lisa made a groundsheet by laying out our packliners and she curled up in one corner.

'Someone should probably keep watch,' Rebecca told us.

'Can't, already asleep,' Jonathon replied, collapsing next to Lisa.

'Do we have to?' I asked.

'Three hours each.' I knew how exhausted she had to be, having led the whole way. And I owed it to them, after being so useless.

'Okay. Who do I wake next?'

'Thanks Marko.' She reached out and touched my arm, just below the elbow, and the feel of it made me want to hold her, or maybe just cry. 'I'll do the next one.'

'No worries.'

I watched her join the others. There was barely room there for the three of them. Lisa was curled up foetus-like at the edge, Jonathon was in the middle on his back, and Rebecca was on the other side, turned into him, using his shoulder as a pillow. All three of them were already asleep. In the first hint of morning it was a picture in need of something more than my memory to capture it. 'Seventh Form PE Trip,' it should have said, a photograph over somebody's fireplace. In that moment of looking on I knew I loved them, all three equally, and the realisation of it threatened to choke me.

I didn't know how I was going to stay awake for another three hours. We were on a terrace above the stream with a steep bank above us, so it was only the way down to the water that needed watching. I sat on a rotting branch and tried focussing on details, the exact structure of a curling frond in front of me, or piecing together a picture of the stream from the sounds it made, gurgling along its shallow bed, the silence of broad pools, the crashing of its tumbling waterfalls. My mind drifted quickly though. All it wanted was to shut down behind closed eyes. I tried standing and then pacing but my legs abused me and anyway there wasn't room.

Finally I resorted to the one thing that might hold back sleep, dragging to the surface images my mind had been trying to bury. Ms Jenkins's last moments alive, and later, finding her body. And all the thoughts that wrapped themselves around those images, thoughts of how I'd failed, how twice I'd let everybody down. Of all the things I might have said or done, instead of hiding there silent, letting it happen. Of the coward I was, not even able to take my share of her weight. It ripped me apart, knowing that, but at least it kept me awake.

Then I discovered something else, something that could ease the pain. I took to imagining how it would be, if I ever met that man again. I didn't have his face, but I had his voice, and a sense of him, enough to play out scenes of revenge inside my head. Each was more horrible than the one before it, and with every dark imagining my load lightened, just a little.

17.

April 23

April 23 (still). My room measures five paces across and four along, not quite a square. Behind the particle board, now I have examined it in detail, the walls are solid concrete block, even the one facing the corridor. The room has been designed as some sort of vault. Now it will be my tomb.

I have been left here to die. It is that simple. I have been that stupid. If this writing is ever found, if you are reading this, you will have already guessed. It wasn't obvious to me though. I was too confident, or too desperate. Not seeing it at all. Not realising how far I am from fully grown, how easy it must have been for them to play me this way.

It could even be funny, if it wasn't for real. Keeping silent all this time, thinking I could plan out the perfect crime, when all the time the perfect crime was already planned. How will it look when they find me? Some wrongly-named patient, mixed up in the confusion of a disaster, his diagnosis well recorded, who fled in an unexplained panic and then was found huddled in a small room on a construction site. All the Doctor has to do is slip back later, when I am dead, and unlock the door. It will seem so obvious then, a simple act of lunacy, sitting here and starving, prisoner only to my inner demons. Not a mark on me. Not a single piece of evidence, not that they will be suspicious enough to look anyway. The Doctor is cleverer than I am. The Doctor has won.

I was feeling so proud of myself, the way I handled Andrew, forced him to keep quiet, got him to lead me here, slipped this writing down the back of my pyjamas without him seeing. But he was playing me. I don't know how he managed to keep such a straight face, stopped himself from saying 'ha, you're so damned stupid'. He was one of them, I'm sure of it. It makes such sense. Watching me the whole time. I hate him for it, but I hate myself more, my stupid, weak, cowardly self.

I don't know what point there is still writing this. What more is there worth saying? I could write of my anger, my frustration, my regret, and now the terror rising up behind all the other emotions, threatening to break over them like a wave. I should write this: 'I don't want to die'. I could try to write it across the walls, give them one last problem to deal with. I don't want to die. I am seventeen and I have done nothing good, just made mistakes. Maybe I've learnt something from them, but what's the point in learning, when time runs out this soon? If I tried to make a list of all the things I've never done I'd be finished before it was. I've never had sex, I've never even been overseas. I've never been in love, I have never felt brave, or certain of anything. I've never found a place where it felt like I belong....

This is going nowhere. I don't have the time. How long can you last without water? Only a few days I think. The Doctor will know. I have no watch so I can only guess at the time. I wrote for a while, enough to take three hours looking at it. Then I rested and waited for Andrew. Then I thought I might slip out for a look around. Then I found the door is locked.

I didn't panic, not at first. Maybe he was just playing safe. He would be back soon. And if the worst happened and he couldn't get back, I could still break my way out. So I looked around more closely. I felt the cold resistance of concrete behind every panel, I noticed the weight of the door. Then I saw how carefully this room had been chosen. Then I panicked.

I haven't just sat round though. I didn't just give up. I scratched away at the concrete with a metal button from my blazer, but it would take years to loosen just one block. I have leapt uselessly at the ceiling and I have hammered and screamed desperately at the door. I even considered charging head first at a wall, to knock myself out cold, do away with the waiting. I couldn't do it though. I am still a coward.

Then I sat in the corner and I strained my mind, looking for the simple solution they always find on television, the cunning plan that is so obvious I am missing it. I sat and I thought and I asked myself questions but when it came to the answers I was empty.

So now I am writing again because it is all I have left. It is better than not writing, it keeps the fear out. I am my story and I will keep my story alive. I will not sleep. I will write it down, all of it. I don't want to die.

18.

I slept through the next three shifts and woke feeling tired, sore, and hungry. It wasn't quite dark and Rebecca made us stay quiet as we took turns going down to the stream to drink. This time Jonathon didn't question her. Somehow, while I was sleeping, the two of them had stopped arguing. We shared out exactly half the scroggin, a small handful each, and Rebecca explained the plan for the night. Although it was obvious we weren't at the river she was sure we hadn't missed it by much. If she was right we had veered off the ridge and come down to the upper reaches of one of the small streams that fed it. She figured we should follow the stream down until it joined the river and then continue as planned, up and over to the next valley and out. I was sure I'd once heard something about never following mountain streams in the bush but I kept quiet.

It began to rain and Rebecca repeated her cutting trick with our packliners so soon we were all decked out in matching orange. Straight away I felt too hot but I figured it was better than freezing. When Rebecca went to pick up Lisa's pack Jonathon appeared at her side.

'Nah, I'll take it tonight,' he said.

'I knew it,' Lisa whispered to me.

'Knew what?'

'Rebecca and Jonathon. I knew it would happen.'

'Oh.'

Lisa was beaming, like it represented some huge break-through. To me it felt more like another complication.

I soon found myself missing their arguing. Now, instead of Jonathon's constant sniping, there was only silence, or whispered exchanges that they didn't share. It didn't take me long to remember why you shouldn't walk down streams. Streams form gorges, suddenly getting deep as sheer rock walls force them to narrow. They also plunge over water-falls, small ones like I'd heard during my watch, and much longer drops too, bouncing off sharp rock walls and tumbling into dark pools at their base. So you are forced to get wet, and take risks clambering down drops of slippery stone. Bruises, broken bones, concussion or worse, and the more you concentrate on staying safe the more drained you become. I'd read it all in a bush survival manual in fourth form Social Studies, when we were meant to be researching historical figures in the library. The book didn't have anything to say on the added dangers of doing it at night. I guess it didn't need saying.

Our feet slipped on smooth stones grown slimy under-water, we were forever misreading crossings, getting half-way only to find the water was too deep or the bank on the other side had run out. At every hazard there was a stop, while a decision was made, and with the rain getting heavier all the time I was beginning to shiver.

We were forced to spend as much time scrambling up into the bush as we were in the stream. Often we had to haul ourselves and each other up near-vertical banks. With Rebecca and Jonathon's new interest in each other I was left to slog it out with Lisa. I quickly became used to the feel of her hand gripping mine, stronger than I expected, and her little grunts of thanks and encouragement. We were making terrible progress. At first it was okay pushing on, believing the broad Tauherenikau Valley would appear around the next corner, but after four hours hemmed in by rock and pummelled by the rain I was past believing we were even headed in the right direction. My thoughts became more and more negative – we would never get out. We were using up the last of our precious energy. We were stupid trying this in the dark. Disaster lay just ahead. When I was out of earshot the others talked about me. They blamed me for Ms Jenkins's death – misery settled on me, becoming almost comfortable. I wallowed in it and dragged my feet, so the others were forced to wait for me more and more. Eventually it became too much for Jonathon, who had gone all night without slagging anybody off.

'Jesus Marko, get it together will you?'

I sat down on the nearest rock in reply.

'Fucken hell,' he muttered.

'Jonathon, you won't make him feel any better,' Rebecca said, speaking like I couldn't hear them, or was too young to understand.

'Okay then, what's wrong?' Jonathon asked.

'What do you think? We've got no food. We're not going to make it out of here. She doesn't even know where we are.'

'Yes she does. She's already said.'

'So how come we still haven't reached the river?'

'I'd like to see you do any better.'

'I'm not saying I could. I just think we should stop pretending everything is alright. It's not alright. We're going to die.' And then I was crying. Pathetic, so now I'm ashamed to write it down. But that's how it happened. That's how I was. I was weak.

'Look Marko.' It was Rebecca and her schoolteacher's voice. 'We know how you feel. But you have to keep going, okay? We don't have any choice. Lisa, what's the time?'

'Almost three.'

'Another three hours then. Can you do another three hours?'

'Maybe.'

'We'll make it to the river by then.'

'We were meant to be out of here by then,' I countered, just like a spoilt child. That's what I was. I wanted a world where if I complained loudly enough someone somewhere would give in and change the rules. I wanted a world that doesn't exist. Someone should have hit me. Jonathon almost did. He was standing over me, so close I could smell the last precious cigarette on his breath.

'Well we're moving on now, you useless fuck, and I don't care whether you come with me or not. I haven't got the energy to save your arse. Got it?' Then to the others. 'Come on, let's go. We've got to keep moving or we'll freeze.'

It worked. It snapped me out of my self-pity.

'Sorry guys,' I called to them as we moved on. The other two didn't answer but Lisa dropped back, put her arm around me and squeezed.

'I'm glad you're here Marko,' she said.

We found the river after another hour of following the stream but it wasn't the same river we'd crossed three days earlier. It was more like a lake now. It had slowly filled and then spilled out over its sides, so the trees on the side were surrounded by water, like some fairy tale swamp. In the darkness it was eerie, the sort of place where you could imagine a hooded figure gliding by in a silent boat. A silent boat to match the other dark silences, because for a river that high it wasn't making any noise. It hardly seemed to be moving. The gurgle from the stream rushing down to join it was the loudest noise. It wasn't a flood. Rain hadn't done this. The earthquake had.

'Damn it,' Jonathon said.

'Probably still rising,' said Rebecca. 'Further down the river turns left, straight through the hills. A gorge must have collapsed. It makes getting out trickier.'

Lisa had already edged into the water, to the left in amongst the trees. Suddenly she shrieked and jumped back-wards.

'What is it?'

'I don't know. Something moved.'

'Where? Show me where. No, exactly. This could be dinner.' Jonathon moved forward, using his lighter as a torch. 'Oh yes, shit that's long.'

'What is it?'

'Mother of an eel. Okay, Marko. Come here. Hold the lighter.'

I did as I was told. The light was pathetic but the eel was so big it didn't matter. It was, as Jonathon had said, a mother.

'Okay, just keep the light over it. If it moves, follow it.'

'What are you doing?'

'I'm going to use this stick to flick it out of the water. If either of you two let it get back in, you're dinner. Okay?'

'How do we stop it?' Lisa asked.

'You get a big rock and you beat its brains out.'

Jonathon edged forward. I could see his concentration and I tried to do the same. The eel glided forward with a swish of its huge tail and I waded after it. I heard the other two picking up rocks, all four of us moving in for the kill.

Jonathon struck. In the darkness I lost sight of it but he definitely got it out of the water. Then chaos as we all searched for our prey before it could slither back to safety.

'Got it! Over here.' Lisa's voice. When we reached her she was already into her work, bringing the rock down on the eel's head.

'Thought you were scared of them,' Jonathon said.

'It's still moving.'

'Try the tail. I think they have nerves in their tail.'

'You try.'

So Rebecca crouched at the other end and the two of them pummelled the creature with clockwork ferocity.

'I think it's dead now,' I said. We stood back. It was a metre and a half long and thicker than my wrist. A lot of eating.

'Okay then, let's get this sucker gutted.' Jonathon's knife was already out.

'What'll it taste like raw?' I asked.

'Don't know. Don't care. I'm lighting a fire.'

'No you're not,' Rebecca told him.

'Come on. Why not?'

'They might see it, or smell the smoke.'

'They're nowhere near here. It's food. We'll never get out if we starve.'

'Please,' Lisa added.

'We should get over the river first,' Rebecca said.

'How? It's got to be way deep in the middle.'

'We can have a fire on the other side.'

'We'll be soaked,' I said, forgetting my promise to myself not to whinge again. 'I'm already cold.'

'Same,' Lisa agreed.

'We'd have a fire,' Rebecca argued. 'It's not light yet, we should keep going. We've got one packliner left. If we put our clothes inside it, inside the pack, and float it across, they'll stay dry.'

'You want us to take our clothes off?' Lisa asked.

'No, I want us to get out of here alive.'

'And I want to get this cooked,' Jonathon added, a bit too keenly. 'Come on, let's do it.' His bag was off, then his polar fleece, then his shirt.

'Leave the underwear on, eh?' Rebecca told him. 'It's not quite that desperate yet.'

We stripped and packed our clothes together in the one non-mutilated bag. Rebecca rolled the end up tightly and stuffed it inside the pack. Jonathon hacked off the eel's head, 'in case it gets any ideas during the crossing' and wrapped it around his neck like some crazy scarf. I tried not to look at the others, but I didn't do too well. It was freezing. I could feel the wind passing through my skin. There was no chance of hanging about.

'You can all swim, right?' Rebecca thought to ask.

'I'm not real good,' Lisa admitted.

'You swim the pack over then. It'll float. Marko, you're a bit of a swimmer aren't you?'

'Yeah.' I used to compete, until the fifth form.

'You help her then. Let's go.'

As always Rebecca led the way, and as was becoming custom, Jonathon was close behind her. I watched their white bodies move jerkily then blur into the darkness. There was a single splash and they were swimming.

'You okay?' I asked Lisa.

'I think so,' she replied, her voice vibrating with the cold. It was the strangest feeling, standing so close, half-naked, almost connecting, the darkness and the danger making it more unreal. Awkwardly I tried to make the moment pass. I reached out, to touch her shoulder, to say 'thanks', and 'it's alright'. She moved, or it was the lack of light, and my hand found her breast, before I realised and pulled away.

'Sorry, I didn't ...' I was too embarrassed to finish the sentence.

'I know. Come on. You have to help me.'

'Use it like a flutter board. I'll swim downstream from you.'

And so there was one more thing to take over my thoughts and drain my energy, one more game of staying alive. The water was icy but I hardly noticed. I was too busy staying afloat, keeping my bearings and worrying about Lisa. She gave in to fear, trying too hard, the way you never should in water. I saw her thrashing about. Her head went under then came back up. She tried to climb right on top of the pack but it would never hold her weight. If it went right under, the water would get in.

'It's okay,' I told her. 'Relax.'

I swam beneath her. 'Turn onto your back. I've got you. Don't even kick. Okay, now just one hand on the pack, I'll swim us in.'

Like I'd practised so many times at the surf club. We were being pulled down by the current. It was stronger than I'd expected and I had to work hard, so by the time we could stand I was fighting for breath.

'Thanks Marko.' Lisa clung to my neck for a moment, before standing up herself. The others were waiting at the edge of the water. Jonathon took the pack and his freezing hands struggled with the buckles.

'Yes, it's still dry!'

We used a jersey of Lisa's as a towel and changed back into our clothes as quickly as we could, but cold and embarrassment made us clumsy. We talked about the swim while we did it, like we were trying to cover up how weird it felt, being naked. I wanted to apologise again, for everything, but Lisa stopped me before I could get going.

'Forget it will you, Marko? You got me across the river. I would have drowned.'

As if that could make everything alright. It didn't, not at all, but I couldn't explain so I stayed quiet.

We built our fire further up in the bush, or at least we watched Jonathon build it. Our only contribution was to yell at him every time he tried to stoke it up, which was all of the time.

'Jesus, just trying to get some heat here.'

We sat around with our underwear hanging off sticks, trying to dry it out. The light of the fire danced over the others' faces, bringing them to life. Jonathon cut the eel into four strips and we followed his lead, wrapping it around a stick and turning it over in the flames.

It was the warmth of the fire. It was the feeling of being safe, on the other side of the river. It was the taste of the food, hot and solid and smoky. It was the other bodies, more real now, beneath their clothes. It was so many things. I've never felt so warm, so in place. I've never felt so much that

I wanted to stay alive. There was only one thing wrong, one thing missing, but none of us mentioned her. Instead Jonathon and Rebecca, who'd both finished their food, stood up together, like it was something they'd planned.

'We, ah, might just go off for a bit of a walk, check out the way for tonight,' Jonathon said, because even here, it still felt best to lie about some things.

'We'll be back soon,' Rebecca said, 'before it's light.'

'Funny isn't it?' Lisa said, when they'd left. We were sitting close. The heat of the fire was enough to make my eyes water. I looked into the flames.

'What?'

'Those two.'

'Suppose.'

We sat in silence, the sort of silence where you can tell there are things that need to be said, pushing in at the edges. Eventually Lisa found the words.

'I still can't believe she's dead.'

'I know.'

'Tell me again, how it happened.'

So I did, and this time it came out different, because the way she was listening was different. This time her face wasn't bruised with the shock of it, trying to block it out, so I didn't have to hurry, or try to make it sound any way in particular. I could just tell it like it was, so it was like being there again, and this time Lisa was there with me. I finished and there was quiet again, quiet filled with remembering.

'Do you think, like, that she knew?' Lisa asked.

'Knew what?'

'That she was dying.'

'It was very quick.'

'Yeah ...'

'I wish I'd done something.' The tears tasted salty in my mouth. 'She didn't even know I was there. She thought she was on her own.'

'You couldn't have done anything,' she said. She put her arm around me but I still couldn't believe her.

That's when Jonathon and Rebecca came back, crashing through the bush.

'Now you two, keep it decent,' Jonathon said, then he saw the tears. 'Oh, sorry man.'

'Nah, it's sweet.' I sniffed.

'It's a bummer.' They sat back down. 'You know what I'd do to those fuckers if I ever got the chance?'

We all had ideas on that, all except for Lisa, who kept her thoughts to herself while we outbid each other with gruesome punishments. The sky lightened and the air filled with the sound of birds coming awake. Rebecca suggested we move further back into the bush and find a place to sleep. She volunteered to put the fire out and do the first watch. This time we found a bigger flat patch to lay out the bags. It didn't feel at all strange when Lisa lay down behind me and folded her body into mine. It wasn't even too weird the way she wrapped her arms around me and kissed my neck. I put my hand over hers and squeezed it and I got this funny feeling, like when you've just seen a great movie and walking out you wish you were one of the people you see lining up to go in, because you'll ever be able to see it like that again. I was still hungry and we were still half lost and there was so much to still be properly frightened of but as exhaustion turned to sleep I had a smile on my face.

That night when we moved off I was beginning to believe we'd make it out. We were close, less than seven hours from the road end according to Rebecca. The river had come up a bit more but seemed to be levelling off. We would climb the next ridge, down to the Waiohine River, and follow it out. It sounded simple, even in the dark. We were all talking again, making jokes and giving each other shit, so different from the thick silence of the night before. Just like four teenagers having some fun in the bush. Like it was over. Like we had beaten it.

It's easy now to say we should have known, but we'd been so careful for so long and careful is exhausting. It's easy to keep yourself from thinking things that should be thought. Things like how dangerous we were to those three men, knowing what we knew, how they might be just as desperate as we were. How, once you've killed someone, what is and isn't reasonable has got to change. Or how much ground you could cover if you travelled by daylight, and had food, and how obvious our path out was. How easy smoke from a morning fire might be to spot.

They were waiting for us, listening to our voices the whole time, tracking us from above. They meant to kill us all, I'm sure of that. I don't know how they thought they'd do it, but suddenly they were amongst us. Lisa screamed first, then Jonathon. It was dark and there were only three of them and whichever way they'd figured it, it was always going to go crazy then.

I get aggressive when I lose my temper. I just go wild. I've always been like that. Mum was the one who decided I should do judo. She thought it might give me some discipline. It didn't work out that way. I heard Lisa's scream and straight off I was there, kicking out hard, down at a knee. In a situation like that it's mostly luck. I must have got lucky because there was a groan and he crumpled. To my left there was another scream, not one of us, and then running. I saw them all, Lisa, Jonathon, and Rebecca, familiar shapes in the darkness, running off together. I had to get with them, but as I moved I felt someone take hold of my ankle.

'Got one,' I heard him shout.

'Where?'

'Here.' Time enough for me to get a fix on his position and stomp on his face. I was free, pumped full of adrenaline and hatred. Disorientated too, with no time to get my bearings. So I ran blindly, hoping it was the right direction, and my ears filled with the sound of crashing feet behind me.

'This way!' my hunter was shouting. 'This way!'

All three of them after me, and then a tree root to help them, so I was tumbling down, and as I hit the ground another weight crushed me from above. My face was in the dirt and his knees were on my back. I felt his bony fingers digging into my neck, trying to choke the life out of me. Not trying to hold me down, not trying to subdue me, trying to end it.

I had no time. The world was on slow motion but not slow enough. You win by surprise, by tricking your opponent into movement you can use. So I didn't try to throw him, or prise his hands from my throat. I reached for his elbow and pulled him forward, and he didn't resist because he wasn't expecting it. As his weight came forward I rolled into his movement and it toppled him. I was on my back but on top of him. I hit out with my elbow, hard where his throat should have been. I heard the gurgle. Not hard enough to kill him, it wasn't a direct hit, but enough to be free. The other two were close, coming on fast as wildly waving torchlight. As I threw myself forward I turned and for a moment we were face to face, just as a torch beam steadied on us.

'There they are!'

I could see only his eyes, filled with hatred and pain. It was him, the one who had killed her. A face I can never forget, staring for that split second into mine. The Doctor.

Then I was up and running again and they must have stopped to check on their friend because I couldn't hear them behind me. I took no chances. I ran until I had no running left in me and then I stumbled on some more. When I stopped I was too exhausted to think of anything.

As my breathing settled, thoughts returned and they were thoughts of hatred. I hated him so much I wanted to turn back and hunt him down, but I knew I'd never find him. I hated him for what he'd done to Ms Jenkins, for what I'd had to see and how it made me feel every time I thought of it. I hated him for all the wishing I had inside of me, wishing that I'd done something more. That was his fault and I hated him for it, just as much as I hated him for the feel of his hands around my throat in the dark, and the look in his eyes. A look that said he would kill me, if he ever got the chance. Most of all though, I hated him for separating me from the people I needed most just then, for leaving me all alone. I needed Jonathon and his smart-arsed mouth, Rebecca and her hard-arsed ways. I needed Lisa and her way of understanding me. I was alone, lost in the bush, with the taste of possible death in my mouth, and for that I hated him most of all.

That hatred got me out. Hating so much that I couldn't let him beat me. Hating him to the point where I could think of nothing else, only getting out and finding him and making him pay. There is a part of me that can't give in, couldn't give in there in the bush, can't give in now, writing this down. I knew I would never get my bearings again in the dark so I decided to sleep again until morning. I made myself as comfortable as I could on some damp moss and hoped it wouldn't rain.

The next morning I felt the weakest I have ever felt. The eel had reacted badly and I had to squat in the bush. When I started to move again my legs almost gave way beneath me. I was dizzy and there was pain in my head and my stomach. My mouth was dry. I knew I had to back-track to the water. I tripped over too many times to remember on the way back down. I reached the river and drank straight from it, kneeling at its edge like an animal. I splashed the cool water over my face, trying to clear my head. I sat down on the side of what was now a small lake and made the following decisions.

I would stick to Rebecca's plan, climb directly up, onto the ridge, then straight down to the Waiohine. I would follow that out to the Wairarapa farmland. Without food any more resting was impossible, it would only use up precious time. No matter how I felt I promised myself I would keep moving. And that was all I decided. It was as far as I could see. Images of the Doctor would keep me moving forward. Somehow, later, I would find him. I even remember feeling pleased, that the others hadn't seen his face, so I might have a chance of getting to him before the police did.

I walked. The details here are hazy. The picture distorts, blurs, then disappears. I walked all day. I remember dark coming on. I remember nausea, and headaches like I have never felt. I remember seeing the Doctor again, as shadows moved and then later as full scale hallucinations took hold. Trees became skyscrapers and I found a Coke machine that was out of order, and followed a pathway of red carpet. Only luck can have kept me from circling about my own death.

I remember a fence, the beginning of farmland. There was grass, and cattle, and I knelt at a water trough.

And then I came awake here, in this hospital. I can guess more now. I must have lain in the paddock a while before I was discovered. I don't believe it was purely coincidence that led me back to the Doctor. He must have known this is where I would end up, if I ever made it out. So he got himself working in the emergency ward, and waited for me. I don't understand why I wasn't identified when I came in. The others must have told people I was still missing. Maybe he found some way of hiding my identity, before he decided to drug me to the point of forgetting. Or maybe the others ...

But I didn't forget. I haven't forgotten. I am starting to lose it now, the ability to place one thought in front of the other. I stop and howl with the fear of being alone again, forever this time, and the sound of it only frightens me more. I stopped taking his drugs. Somehow I stopped taking his drugs. Another chance was thrown to me. Too late now though. I am dying.

19.

April 24

I was dying. I felt that final fear creeping up through my bones. The Doctor's crime was close to complete, close to perfect. But he lost his nerve. He grew scared I suppose, paranoid, the deed grew too large for him. He came back to the room, to check up on me, to finish a job that was finishing itself.

I heard the lock turning and by then I was so sweaty weak with fear I wasn't even sure it was real. I saw the door come slowly open and I took my chance to stay alive. I was lying in the corner, my back against the wall, this book and the plaited pillowcase hidden behind me. I didn't move, but let my eyes half-open and follow him into the room. He closed the door and locked it. He stood, as far away from me as was possible in the small space, and watched me carefully. I watched him back. He was dressed for the weekend, jeans and ski jacket. His face looked older than I remembered, the skin hung more loosely and there was darkness beneath his eyes. I realised this was the first time I had been able to look at him properly. I searched his eyes for the monster that lurked there but they were empty. Blank. I wondered what he was doing. I tried to anticipate him. There would be a moment. A single chance. I tried to find some strength, awaken my muscles without moving.

The Doctor pulled a syringe from his pocket.

'You can hear me, can't you Marko?' he said, speaking softly, like any Doctor to any patient. I nodded and made a noise in the back of my throat.

'This won't hurt at all. You'll just fall asleep. You must be tired.'

And if I close my eyes, and imagine hearing that same voice in a different place, it is almost possible to imagine that in some sick way he actually cared. That he wanted to make it easy. I watched him carefully, not trying to understand, trying to anticipate. He held the syringe up in front of him, checking it against the light. He stepped forward and I made as if to move away, but only weakly, like a person past resisting. I had one end of the pillow-case in my hand. My chance. Not yet though. He was moving too methodically, too carefully, as if ready for me to strike.

'You don't have to kill me,' I croaked, watching his eyes for a reaction. They clouded with a sudden sadness, taking me by surprise, and I had to force myself to look past them, keep watching, waiting.

'I'm not killing you Marko. I wanted you to live. That was my plan. I saved you, you know. You were half-dead when they brought you in, I helped stabilise you.'

The hand that held the syringe fell back to his side, as if his mind was floating off the task. There were things he wanted to say, and I would help him drop his guard.

'You're killing me now.'

'Not me Marko, circumstance.'

He said it like they were old familiar words, an argument he'd had a hundred times before. I watched him and tried not to listen. 'It's what gets us all in the end. In different circumstances, it'd be you killing me. If you have to blame someone, blame Nurse Margaret. She was the one who had to know best, who had to experiment with your dosage, against my instructions. If she'd stayed out of this, you'd still be alive.'

'I am still alive.'

'Yes, you're right. This has taken long enough.'

I pushed myself up off the wall, still sitting but leaning forward towards him, as if I was desperate, as if it was all I had left. I've never been much of an actor but I could see that he'd bought it. He didn't even step back from me.

'Why did you do it? Why did you kill her?'

'It was an accident. That's all.' He looked away from my stare. 'They happen. This isn't personal.'

He took my arm and again I was soft in my resistance. He moved his full weight on to me, his back against my chest, holding me down like a shearer pinning a stroppy sheep. I waited. The moment would come when he checked for a vein, a professional lost in procedure. I could feel his weight relax against me. I had no idea how much strength I had left.

I pulled my arm over his head as quickly as I could manage, whipping the rope around his neck and grabbing the loose end with my free hand. I was weak and it was a clumsy movement but again I had surprise. He hadn't learnt so much. When his hands came up it was to get at the fabric, to relieve the choking. His weight came off me and I knelt up behind him, leaning back on the ends of the crossed over choker, and brought my whole weight to bear on his fragile neck.

It was messier than it should have been. He bucked about frantically. He was much stronger than I was and I held on like a rider at a rodeo, pitting the last of my endurance against his, knowing that without air he would soon lose the battle. As he became calmer I tightened the grip, alert to any tricks. I could have killed him then, but my hatred ran deeper than my rage. He didn't deserve anything quick.

I kept leaning on the rope, maybe for a full minute, till he was sagging against it, close to passing out. Then I pushed him forward, face hard against the concrete floor. I knelt on his shoulder blades and brought one arm up behind his back, locking his wrist with my left hand, pulling his chin back with my right.

'If you try to move,' I told him, 'I will break your arm first, then your neck.'

'No, you can't,' he gasped. 'I never meant for any of this to happen. I beg you. I'll come with you to the police. I'll tell them everything.'

I didn't say a thing. There was nothing I could say that would add to my pleasure. I let his face fall back to the floor and searched his pocket, finding the key. A simple plan was forming. It was what he deserved.

Moving quickly, so he didn't have time to react, I tied one end of the rope around the hand I held. He tried to buck me then but I was ready. I grabbed a handful of his hair and smashed his face down hard. Then I passed the rope around his throat and brought his other hand up to meet the first. Another knot and he was well caught. I could hear him struggling to keep his airway clear. I stood back, safe from him at last. He wriggled onto his side, to return my stare.

I expected him to kick out as I removed his shoes and socks, and then his trousers, but his spirit had crumpled without much of a fight. The trousers weren't a perfect fit but with the ends rolled up they would do. I buttoned up the blazer and ripped the logo off. I must have looked odd dressed that way, but not as odd as being in hospital pyjamas. Still I didn't speak. I was beginning to feel light-headed, not with weakness but with victory. I searched his pockets again and found his wallet. I took sixty dollars, all he had.

'You can't leave me here,' he tried. 'No, don't do that.'

Then he tried screaming, a sound so low and pitiful I had to gag him. My pyjama pants did the job well enough.

I took the syringe and put it in my blazer pocket. I picked up my book and this pen. I was ready to leave the hospital.

'We get what we deserve,' was all I said as I closed the door. I got one last look at his eyes and it wasn't fear I saw there, it was hope, desperate hope. That will fade, and then he will feel the things I have felt.

I walked back out into a different world. Things I'd hardly noticed when Andrew had led me there seemed obvious now. I wandered half-finished corridors, empty of people and sound. I passed a roughly boarded-over lift shaft and then a dark passage without electricity, where cords for light fittings poked down from the ceiling. Twists and turns, a dungeon at the end of a maze, even a 'keep out' tape stretched across the corridor now, at the place where it met the main building. The Doctor should never *have panicked. They wouldn't have found me alive. They won't find him.*

A nurse stopped me as I tried to find my way back through the wards.

'You can't go through there,' she told me, but she said it with a smile and it made me think of Lisa.

'Sorry,' I said. 'I've got myself a bit lost.'

'What are you looking for?' she asked. A normal conversation between two normal people. I was free.

'The cafeteria.'

'Oh, well you're way off then. Go along here, to the lift, and take it down to the ground floor. From there follow the signs through to reception, it's signposted from there.'

'Okay, thanks.'

'No problem,' and another smile. Killing people, it's easier than you might think.

The cafeteria was empty. I could see through the windows it was light outside. Nine-thirty, according to the clock. I bought food and drink, lots of drink, two of the largest juices they had. The woman behind the counter smiled. I wasn't the best dressed person she would see that day but maybe I wasn't the worst either. I took the food outside and walked two blocks to a park before I stopped to eat. The day was bright and it hurt my eyes. I ate slowly. I felt far better than I'd expected to. I thought of the Doctor and a smile rose up through my chest.

I am on a bus now, heading home. The other passengers must wonder at my smile. Maybe to them I just look crazy. I haven't rung ahead. They don't know I am coming. I want to surprise them. I want a chance to practise my story too,. on Mum and Duncan, who won't ask too many questions. I can hardly wait. I am only writing this to stop myself from looking up, from seeing how unbearably slowly we are moving. They're only kilometres away now. They must think I'm dead. Everybody must think I'm dead. But here I am, alive, and with a story to tell that I can hardly believe myself.

Not that I will be telling it, not at first anyway. I have been thinking this over. Only Jonathon, Rebecca, and Lisa can ever know. If they're still alive. I am sure they are. I can feel it. They're the only people who I can trust to understand. And not yet. Not until it is over, and I am sure he is dead. Rebecca might want to take over otherwise, and Jonathon would insist on going for a look, and maybe a spot of torture. So I will have to wait some more. That's alright, I am used to waiting. They will be so surprised, that I have finally done something right. It will be my gift to them.

So it is over. We have reached the place where the road is only half-built and it is getting too bumpy for writing. I have nothing left to say anyway. I have won. I am home. Good things lie ahead, waiting for me.

20.

April 26

Remember how it is when you're little and you've been looking forward to Christmas ever since school broke up? Only now it's happened. It's Christmas night. The food's all been eaten and it's made you feel sick. The new game for your Playstation isn't as good as the TV promised and anyway, everyone else is much better at it than you are. Your grandparents arrive late, with a present meant for someone half your age, and you don't have any words for all your disappointments. So all you can do is cry. Then your Mum says 'It's been a big day. You're tired', but that's not it at all. The presents are crap, nothing's ever as good as you think it's going to be and it serves you right for wasting all that time looking forward to it.

Well it has been a big day. It's been two big days in fact, but that isn't the problem. I'm exhausted but I'm too old to just break down and cry every time it gets too hard, so I'm staying here in bed this morning and I'm doing the only thing that still feels right. I'm writing it down.

Nothing was how it should have been. I walked up from where the bus stops, but not through any city I knew. I was expecting it to be a mess I suppose, but no matter how you prepare yourself it

148

will still be the details that trip you up. A favourite shop that isn't there any more, because it was built too close to a bank; a house still standing, looking perfect, while just across the road another one has gone completely. The view, looking back down over the harbour, where so much is missing you can hardly recognise the bits that are left. And everywhere machinery, bulldozers and cranes, the sounds of new ripping and tearing, of a whole city burying its memories.

It was the shock, the strangeness and familiarity all in one, and being so close to home, because suddenly all the feelings of weakness my body was owed came back. The short climb up to our street became a mountain and I had to cling to the old wooden rail that should never have survived an earthquake to stop myself from slipping back.

Our house looked okay from the road. The whole street seemed to have got off lightly. I found the front door locked and walked round to the back. Then I saw the damage. The conservatory Dad had spent so long on before he walked out, had collapsed. The tent we take up to Ohope every year was set up in the back yard, using most of the space. A tent in a camp site in the middle of summer can look like the most inviting place in the world, but cramped on your back lawn it looks sad and desperate.

The back was locked up too, with a thick chain and a padlock, and when I called out no one answered. It was like I wasn't there at all, like I had become invisible.

So I sat down on one of the green plastic chairs we use for barbecues and I waited, and I felt a whole new set of fears creeping over me. Not how it was meant to be. Not why I wore such a *wide smile when I stepped off that bus.*

I was asleep when Duncan found me. I woke to him shaking me, his bug-eyed face almost exploding, the veins on his neck bulging out as he screamed. It was evening.

'Mum! Mum! Marko! It's Marko! Marko's here!'

Then she was there, clumsy in her running, before stopping dead, like there was a wall between us, and just staring. Then there was laughing and crying and holding too tightly, and cry-ing again. There was so much to say that nowhere seemed the right place to start, and all that came out was half-questions and broken exclamations. Eventually Mum calmed down enough to find her key and we all went through to the lounge where we sat and stared at each other, like none of us spoke the same lan-guage.

'Oh,' Mum kept on saying, then she'd smile strangely and look at me as if I was something she couldn't quite believe in, or she'd go into another round of howling. And I'd say 'it's good to be back', and it was, but not exactly. It wasn't the way I wanted it to be. It wasn't the normal I'd been missing, and that made me want to howl too. Mum got it together long enough to go to the phone and ring Uncle Bruce, to tell him the news and ask him to ring all the other people who needed to know.

Eventually being thirteen got the better of Duncan and he launched into all his earthquake stories, stories he'd told so many times before, the edges were smooth. That got Mum angry. We weren't supposed to be talking about that now, she said. This was supposed to be a happy time. So we sat silently again, be-cause none of us could think of much that was happy to say.

Then the questions came, questions that had to come eventually, but which I still wasn't properly ready for. They told me the others had all come out together a week and a half before, and they were sure I was lost, or ... they didn't say the word. There had been searches. Where had I been? What had happened? I told them all the half-lies that had to be told. I escaped. I became lost, wandered, caught another eel, found some food in a hut. I finally came out over on the west coast. I found a farm house but there was no one there and no phone I could see. I took some money, and some clothes, and caught a bus down. It felt shabby, telling them those stories, the two most important people in the world, and the more I told the more it felt like I was only visiting, like it wasn't my home at all.

Later on Mum sent Duncan off to bed. I knew why she'd done it, what she wanted to say, but she circled around it for a while first. She reeled off lists of people we knew who'd lost their homes, and people whose names I sort of recognised who had died ... a couple of kids from school but no one from my form. She talked about how good people had been, and how hard it was at first, not knowing. Her hair looked greyer to me, and her face hung more heavily on its bones. She told me there were still problems with the electricity, and how the phones weren't reliable. Then she stopped and took a breath, and looked at me more closely.

'Of course they've all been around here, Rebecca and Jonathon and Lisa. They're lovely aren't they?'

Yes, I nodded, they are.

'They've told me of course, about what happened, what you saw. The police have been here too. They'll want to talk to you.'

I knew that. I nodded again.

'And her parents too. The others have been to see them. They would like to see you too I think, if you think you can, when you're ready.'

Another nod. Yes, yes, yes. All things I had expected. All things I would get through.

'There was a lovely funeral Marko. I went along. I thought I should. They haven't found the body. It must be so hard for them.' She stopped then, like a person hurrying through a city who suddenly realises they're lost. Her face looked puzzled, then worried. She stood and walked over to me and leaning down pulled my head close to hers, and tightly gripped my back, as if she was frightened of falling.

I looked past her, to the familiar wall braced now with an unfamiliar iron girder. I knew then this wasn't a beginning. It was the middle of something else I had come back to, and I was too tired to think how that might be.

I stood up myself and hugged her back, but as much as I loved her and as much as I'd looked forward to holding her it didn't feel real. It felt as if my arms might pass right through her if I squeezed too hard. So I told her I loved her and asked her if I would be able to ring Jonathon.

Uncle Bruce rang back first, to tell Mum that the police wanted to send someone round straight away, to interview me, but Mum told him to put it off till the morning. I got through to Jonathon first time. I had to look his number up in the book. His was the only surname I remembered.

'Fuck, Marko!' he said when he heard me. Then he thought

about it for a moment more. 'Fuck, Marko!'

It was worth a scream. Then I had to wait while his end of the phone was crowded out with half-conversations.

'Yes, it is him. He's alive. I don't know, he hasn't said. His place maybe. No, I don't know that either okay? Look, let me talk to him first will you? Sorry about that man, it's just everyone's been so ... Fuck, Marko! How are you? Are you alright?'

'Yeah. Yeah I am.'

'So what happened? I thought they'd got you.'

'Nah, I got away.'

'But you saw them, right? You must have seen their faces. Have you talked to the police?'

'They're coming round tomorrow.'

'Good, good.'

'So, ah, how are you?'

'Yeah, you know. Alright. Bit rough coming back. Have you rung any of the others?'

'Nah, you're first.'

'I can ring them, if you want. Tell them.'

'Yeah, okay.'

'Ah, we should get together eh? You can come round here. How about tomorrow night?'

He said it like he was inviting me to a party. It felt wrong. It was like he was meant to be saying different things, although I didn't know what.

'Um, sure. Suppose so.'

'Be good for Lisa. You heard about her, eh?'

'What? No.'

'Yeah. Awful. Her little brother was one of the ones killed. She's, well you know, how you would be. I'll see if I can get her to come round though. I mean, fuck, Marko!'

'Yeah.'

I wanted to say more but not like that, not down the phone, with Mum still waiting in the background. It would be different the next night, going round, seeing them. And Lisa's brother. That threw me. Jonathon was having another conversation at his end.

'Yeah, I know you are, but it's Marko isn't it? Okay, okay. Hey look, sorry man, I have to go okay?'

'Nah, that's alright.'

'Tomorrow then, seven?'

'Yeah, yeah for sure.'

'Right, bye.'

'See ya.'

'I bet he was relieved,' Mum said, when I'd hung up.

'Yeah. You didn't tell me Lisa's little brother had died.'

'Oh yes, I forgot, somehow. There's just been so much.'

'I should ring. I should have got her number off Jonathon. You don't know her surname do you?'

'No. There was something about you all in the paper but I don't think I've kept it.'

I tried Jonathon again but the phone wouldn't connect. Neither could I. Maybe tomorrow it would be better, I thought. Maybe tomorrow would be real.

'Look, ah, I'm tired as. I might just go to bed.'

'Oh yes, of course, you just ... oh dear.' Mum put her hand to her mouth, horrified that she'd only just thought of it. 'A doctor.

We need to take you to a doctor.'

'No, no,' I assured her. 'I'm fine, honestly. It hasn't been so bad. I just need sleep, that's all.'

'If you're sure.'

'I am.'

'Well, as long as you're alright.' She hugged me again. 'I'll try to ring your father again. Bruce wasn't able to get hold of him.'

I lay awake for hours, staring at the shadows on the ceiling. I tried to think of the dying Doctor. I tried to enjoy all the feelings of victory I had promised myself but there was nothing there. I felt empty and cheated.

The police came round early the next morning. My cereal bowl was still wet with milk and my mind was still fuzzy with bad sleep. Mum tried to hover in the background but they asked her to leave us alone. They seemed eager to get on with it. They were both in plain clothes, a bald one with a moustache and a coat he didn't take off and a younger thinner man in a navy suit, who wrote everything down and never smiled.

The interview dragged. They wanted to know everything and kept getting snagged on the tiniest, most unimportant details. I just wanted them to leave. There was no work for them here. It was already sorted. The bald one kept on saying 'You know how important it is don't you?' like there was some chance I might not have worked that out. Like I hadn't been there. I worked through it one slow detail at a time, being honest as much as I could, but always avoiding the truth.

They didn't hide their disappointment when it got to the attack in the dark, where I got split from the others. I could tell they'd been saving that bit up, like they hoped they'd find all the answers there. But it was dark, I told them. I was panicked, and tired and confused, and no, I didn't see any faces. I didn't see anything new.

They lost interest then. They asked me more, about where I went then and how I got out, and I told my lies again. They came easier, now I'd practised them. They weren't listening that closely anyway. The thin one had stopped writing. I don't think they got much. Later, when the Doctor is found dead and questions are asked, they won't have anything to make a link between a patient who ran away and a boy who got lost in the bush.

There were other visitors during the day, friends of the family mostly, but I was fidgety and found it hard to concentrate. Probably I was rude to them but there were lots of understanding smiles. Mr Camden called round, just for a minute, to bring back my bike and tell me how pleased everyone was that I was safe. He made a joke about how I'd have lots to write in my assessment journal. He's a good guy.

There was a journalist from the paper with a photographer in tow but I got Mum to make them go away. I'm not that stupid. Jonathon rang again, to say hi and give me directions to his place. Seven o'clock, too long to wait. I so needed to see them. Seeing them would make me feel better.

I watched some television to try to make the time go faster but the programmes all annoyed me. Around five there was another knock at the door. Mum had gone down to the supermarket and Duncan was round at a friend's place. Apparently it was Sunday. I thought about ignoring whoever it was until they got sick of knocking and went away but a part of me knew who it would be and I couldn't leave them standing.

They were both in their forties. They looked awkward and formal and as much as I stared I couldn't see any of their daughter in their faces. I led them through to the lounge. They started off by apologising and they meant it. They told me how glad they were I was alright and they meant that too. Mr Jenkins has the sort of face that can carry a lot of meaning. It's long, flanked by bushy grey sideburns, and deep lines run either side of his mouth. He is tall, even sitting down. He didn't slouch at all, but sat upright on the edge of his seat, and when he wasn't speaking he would stare straight at me and nod. Mrs Jenkins was shorter and more interested in the clutter of our lounge. When I looked at her I saw all the pain and confusion that Mr Jenkins had somehow managed to hide.

'I know how hard it must be for you, Marko,' Mr Jenkins said. He'd been using my name from the moment we met. 'But the others tell us you were there, that you saw Carol die. We need to know, you see. We need to hear it. Please, tell us how it happened.'

A story should blunt with the retelling. By the fourth time there should be a distance, you shouldn't still be right there, in the middle of the things you're describing. I was though. The story I told them was a story filled with pain and sadness and empty of meaning and as I told it I saw the way they were both still struggling to understand. When I finished there was a tear on my cheek and Mr Jenkins was still staring, still nodding, like the words were still sounding inside his head.

'So in a way it was an accident,' he said, with an emphasis on the 'was', as if it was something he'd believed all along.

'He meant to hit her,' I told him. 'He was angry.'

'But,' he stopped, like he was straightening a picture inside his head. 'Her head hit the tree you think? And she fell, and they thought she was dead straight away? It was the head then, against the tree. I'm sorry, but without a body you see, there's nothing anyone else can tell us, and we do need to know.'

'Yes,' I agreed, 'it was the tree, but ...'

'An accident. In a way.'

'No, Malcolm. Let him finish. You said but. But what?'

'Well, I was just going to say it wasn't an accident was it? He hit her and she died. He meant to hit her.'

'Yes,' she replied. 'That's the thing I don't understand. Why? Why was he so angry? What did he want from her? Was it some sort of misunderstanding, do you think? Why wouldn't they just let her go? I don't understand.'

'Sandra, don't. We've been through this with the police, and the others. We can't know what they were thinking. It was one of those things, a moment that went wrong. There's no point speculating. It won't do us any good. And it's not fair on Marko. He doesn't know either.'

But I did know. I knew more than I was saying. I heard their voices, the way they talked. I saw his hand on her breast. I saw myself too, just watching, not yelling out, not helping at all. I know what he is, the Doctor, I know he's a killer, same as I know where he is and how he's suffering now. So many things I knew but couldn't tell, sitting there across from them, knowing too that *nothing I could say would make it better.*

'Maybe they'll catch them,' I said. 'Then we might know some more. Then they might get what they deserve.'

They looked at me, then at each other, like this was something they'd already spent a lot of time talking about.

'No,' Mrs Jenkins told me, shaking her head. 'That wouldn't help. That wouldn't help at all.'

They both stood up and Mr Jenkins thanked me again. He shook my hand before he left and Mrs Jenkins thought about hugging me but changed her mind. She was right. She hardly knew me at all.

I was the first one round to Jonathon's. He didn't hug me either, but we both hesitated before deciding against it. Back in the bush we would have. Maybe if he'd known about the hospital we would have too. I'd decided on the way over I was going to tell them about the Doctor, as soon as they asked. I needed someone else to know.

The pizza Jonathon had ordered arrived but not the others.

'Rebecca'll be late on purpose,' Jonathon told me. 'To make sure she doesn't have to spend time alone with me.'

'Not going so well then?'

'No, I pissed her off somehow. It wasn't my fault though. It was never going to last. It was a bush thing. It's different back here, you know?'

'Yeah.'

Jonathon told me more about the things I'd missed. About Ms Jenkins's funeral and how they still had a coffin, and a burial, even though they never found the body. (They found something *though, where we said, but they're not saying. You know how the police can be.) He told me how the whole school had been there, and hundreds of other people too, and even though it had only been one funeral in the middle of so many, how the TV and newspaper reporters all showed up and it made the news. He told how Mr Jenkins gave a speech and although it was 'quite amazing' he couldn't remember much about it. (Have you met him? He's quite intense isn't he?) Jonathon said that the three of them were told they could say something at the funeral if they wanted, but Lisa was too beaten up, with her brother, and Jonathon didn't want to, and Rebecca wouldn't if she was the only one. It was what they'd argued about. (But you know, I didn't know her, so what could I say? There were all those people there who were really really sad and I didn't want to get up there and just pretend.) I asked how Lisa's brother had died but he wasn't too sure (earthquake shit, something collapsed.) He was just starting to ask me about my whole adventure, and I was thinking of ways to block him, when Rebecca arrived.*

Rebecca did hug me. Just a short one, as soon as she walked in, like she'd thought about it in advance.

'How are you?' she asked.

'Yeah, alright. You know.'

'I'm so pleased you got away. I mean, I was so scared that … well, we all were. Did Jonathon tell you we went back to look for you?'

'Nah.'

'Typical.'

'Thanks for doing it, though.'

'No worries. Did you hear they moved the body somewhere? They had dogs in and everything but they couldn't find it.'

'I reckon they cut her up.'

'Jonathon!'

'No, I do. How else did they move her? A little bit in each pack and ... ow, what was that for?'

'For being you.'

'There's pizza left. You might want to microwave it.'

'Get a vegetarian?'

'I forgot.'

'Wanker.'

And then they were fighting again, half-hassling, half-joking, like we'd been transported back in time. Like nothing had happened. They started on school gossip next. Any other time it might have been alright, not then. I tried to join in and kept one eye on the door, waiting for Lisa to arrive. Then I could tell them. Then it would all be different. Then we'd all have to stop pretending.

It was just after nine when she finally arrived, not looking all that much like Lisa. Same face, same hair, even clothes I recognised from school. Different eyes though, and a different way of holding me.

'Marko,' she whispered. 'I'm so glad.' But there wasn't much gladness left in her.

'Hey, I'm so sorry to hear about your little brother.' I'd forgotten to ask the others his name. 'I was going to ring you last night but the phone's been dodgy.'

'That's okay. Thanks.'

And then silence. A careful silence, like any step now could be *in the wrong direction. It was up to Lisa to lead the way.*

'So where's the pizza?' she asked, with a smile that looked like a lie to me. 'Hey, is this movie just starting? I wanted to see this.'

Her way of saying 'I don't want to talk' and if Lisa didn't want to then we wouldn't. It was her call. So I sat there, close to the others at last but still a world away, with stories of hospitals and Doctors and killing trapped inside of me while the TV told some other story I couldn't much believe in.

I looked up at Lisa a few times, curled up at the end of the couch. I tried to catch her eye but she was locked on the screen, out of harm's way. Rebecca finally asked me, in the ad break, with only fifteen minutes of the movie left.

'So how did you get out, anyway?'

'I already told you,' Jonathon said.

'I want to hear it properly.'

Properly, but in under four minutes, so there was nothing to do but trip through the lie I had built; fighting clear, running, eel, hut, more food, farmhouse, bus. Then the ads finished. No time for questions. As soon as the film was over Lisa stood up.

'I should be going, get back to the family,' she explained. 'It's been good seeing you all though. A bit of time out, you know. Marko, come here. I am so pleased ...' She hugged me again.

'I'll ring you eh?' I said.

'That'd be good. You should come round. I'm not back at school yet.'

She smiled, gave the others a little wave, and left.

'Shit, that must be so hard,' Rebecca said. 'Wish there was

something we could do.'

So did I.

So it's been a big two days. Then there was last night, making it even bigger.

I've had nightmares before, or bad dreams I thought were nightmares. I remember times when I was little, running into Mum and Dad, asking if I could sleep with them. Last night wasn't like that. Last night wasn't the sort of nightmare you can fix by sitting up and turning on the lights. It's stupid but I'm even scared to write it down, as if putting it on paper means it will still be here, in the room with me. Stupid because of all the real things I've seen, things I've already written down. But nightmares are worse somehow. They do things to your mind when your mind can't defend itself.

I dreamed I woke up and I was here in my room. The walls were darker, stained wood took the place of wallpaper, and they rose up high so I couldn't see the ceiling, but I was still here. It was still my room. Looking up I felt as if I was at the bottom of something, as if I had fallen. There was no door but I hardly noticed that, as if I didn't expect there to be. It was this room and I was in this bed and something had woken me up.

A sound. I sat up and listened. It was at the window, not tapping or knocking but a gentle, irregular bumping sound. I got up and the feeling of the cold floor on my feet was real enough to penetrate the dream so I woke a second time. Still, I needed to check the window, to be sure, before I went back to sleep.

I pulled back the curtain and the blackness beyond the glass was unfamiliar, too thick to be the city by night. A bubble formed against the pane and rose up. Water. It was water. I followed the bubble and saw the Doctor there, floating. Not moving but not lifeless either, his face glowing white, his eyes looking past me, into the room, filled with longing. There was no acknowledgement, no recognition, he just hung there, and when the current moved him he came forward. His face bumped into the glass and his bloated features squashed against it, as if he was made of rubber.

I wanted to run but there was nowhere to go. I tried to pull the curtains closed, to hide his face, but the curtains were gone. I was stuck there, staring at him. Then the look in his eyes changed, from longing to panic, and I saw the fingers on one hand curl slowly, as if it took his every effort to move them, so that he was pointing at my feet.

I looked down to see they were already covered in water, and the water was so dark it was as if I was dissolving in it. At the place where the water touched the wall the wall was dissolving too. Soon I would be with him, floating on the outside, unable to break in.

I screamed. I opened my mouth and filled my lungs and bellowed, aware I was still dreaming and desperate to wake myself. But there was no sound. The water kept coming until I was floating too and that was the most frightening part of all, the feeling of nothing. No weight, no strength, no movement. It was like no other dream I've ever had, it did not progress and it did not end. I was stuck there, suspended for a time that lasted forever. Sometimes I would bump against the Doctor, sometimes into one of the many windows that now surrounded me.

When I woke up this morning I was exhausted. I never want another night like that. Can he be doing this to me, from where he is, trapped and dying? I know that's not possible but I also know how easy it is to know things that are wrong. Now I can't even leave this bed, because I don't know where to go. I don't know what to do next.

I have to tell someone. I have to be rid of part of this. Maybe Lisa. She said it herself last night. She said I should call round. It might be good for her to hear it. It might cheer us both up.

21.

April 27

I'd got Lisa's address off Jonathon the night before. Her phone number too but I didn't ring. I didn't want to hear 'now's not a good time'. I couldn't stay in the house any longer. I knew the street, up in Karori, not that far from us. I took my bike.

It was a big house, dark brick and new-looking, with a smooth twisting driveway and a black iron gate pulled open. Not the sort of place where you'd expect much could go wrong, just looking at it. I leaned my bike against a bush and then changed my mind, wheeling it to the side of the double garage. I rang the doorbell. I waited. It was good to be out of the house but I felt nervous, being there.

'Yes, hello?' It had to be her mother. Young, with big eyes. Good-looking. Sad.

'Hello. Ah, I'm Marko. I've just come round to see Lisa, if that's alright.'

'Marko? Oh yes, of course. Marko. I was so glad, I mean we were all so glad, to hear you were safe.'

'Yeah, um, sorry to hear about Matthew.' My good luck and her bad luck stared at each other for a moment. 'Um, is Lisa in?'

'Oh, no, look you've just missed her. She's gone up to the cemetery.'

'Makara?'

'Yes.'

'Do you think she'd mind if I went there?'

'She'll tell you if she does.' She saw my bike. 'Be careful going out. They've had to change the road, down through the farm on the right. It's very bumpy. There are signs of course. A lot of people are using it now.'

I counted twenty cars in the carpark. To the left on a freshly-mown hill was the earthquake section, rows of new dirt marked out by small, in-the-meantime undertakers' plaques, all looking the same. A woman walked past me with flowers. She smiled at my lost expression, as if to show she understood. Some people were sitting, others stood, looking like the statues they have in older cemeteries. Others fretted about, trying to find ways of stopping their flowers from blowing on to the wrong graves. I couldn't see Lisa. I thought of looking for his name, Matthew Harding, eleven, but it didn't seem right to walk through all that sadness like a tourist. It didn't feel right standing there staring either. I was going to leave. I felt fear turning to panic again, tightening my skull. I tried to relax, let the attack pass, but it was lodged there. I needed to see Lisa so badly I almost screamed out her name. Then I heard her, somewhere behind me.

'Marko!'

There was a steeper bank, just before the grass gave way to gorse, overlooking the graves. She was sitting there, sheltering from the wind. I walked over, having to stop myself from running, and sat down. I realised I was smiling and stopped.

'What are you doing here?' she asked.

'Looking for you. Your mum said this was where you were. You don't mind do you?'

'No, of course not. It's good to see you. Mum doesn't like coming here much, not yet. Dad neither. Liz's gone back to Auckland. It's good to have some company.'

She moved closer, right up against me, and rested her head on my shoulder. It could have been the bush again. I felt my panic retreating.

'Awful isn't it?' she said, looking out at the carefully measured plots.

'Yeah.'

'Too much dirt. I mean, you know what it is right, you know it's a grave, so it shouldn't matter, but it's just too obvious like that. I can't wait until the grass grows. I was thinking of getting some seeds. Do you think they'd be allowed?'

'Probably just blow on to the next one.'

'Like the flowers.' She smiled. 'I think I'd want to be buried down that end, where the wind blows. You get a lot of flowers down there.'

'Where is he? Matthew. Where's he buried?'

'Second row, three in from this side. Sounds like a school photo doesn't it?'

'Are you alright? I mean, you know …'

'Yeah, I guess. I mean, no, not really. I don't know. I don't even know what alright is, most of the time. I feel like shit, but only when I'm awake, you know. That's how I want to feel though. I don't want to feel okay. I don't want it to be like nothing's happened. Mum wants us all to see a grief counsellor but I'm not sure about that. It would be like letting a stranger in. How about you? We didn't talk so much last night. Sorry. How are you? Are you okay?'

'Yeah, I am,' I lied. I knew it was the time to tell it, but I was afraid to start. They weren't the sort of words you could ever take back. 'Well sort of. There's something I need to tell you. No one knows this. No one can know. You have to promise. You have to say you'll never tell.'

'What is it?'

'Promise, please.'

'What's it about?' she asked.

'Up in the bush. The guy who killed Ms Jenkins. It's good news really. You'll be pleased. But you can't tell. You have to promise.'

She looked me in the eye.

'Yeah, I guess.' She didn't even sound that interested. She sounded tired. 'I promise I won't tell.'

I started slowly, unsure of my footing, expecting her to interrupt. She didn't though, and I kept going, so soon I was lost in the telling of it, while relatives came and went and the wind blew and flowers were scattered about. I told her about tripping over, about fighting free, and seeing his face. I told her about the hospital, the drugs he gave me, Margaret who I should have trusted, Andrew who fooled me, this book where it's all written down. It came out in a rush and with the words came the feelings. Suddenly it all seemed so much clearer again. I was the victim. I was angry. I was right. I had won; for me, for Ms Jenkins's family, for Lisa and the others. After everything that had happened, the words were surrounding me, wrapping me in their blanket. The weight was lifted. It would be alright now. I wanted to take Lisa in my arms, thank her for sitting there and listening, letting it all come out. Almost as much as I wanted her to turn towards me and tell me how amazing I was, for doing what I had done. There are so many different kinds of stupid, and that was mine.

'You're just so lucky to still be alive,' she finally said.

'I know.'

'And it was the day before yesterday, when you left him?' she checked. Her face was screwed up, like she was having trouble taking it in.

'Yeah.'

'So he'll still be alive.'

'Not for long,' I said, not seeing where she was headed. There was a pause. Then she said it, quiet and determined, and the whole world moved beneath me one more time.

'You know what you have to do, don't you Marko?'

No way. I shook my head. She was there too. She saw the body. She'd been attacked, right alongside me in the night. She could have been killed just as easily. She couldn't think it, it wasn't possible. I wanted to get on my bike and pedal away, before I had to hear her say the words.

'You've got to let him go.'

'Why?' I heard myself say. I was shaking and my mouth was dry. She was shaking too. It wasn't fair, that we should have to do this. We weren't that old.

'Look out there,' she told me. 'Isn't it obvious? The world doesn't need any help dealing out its shit, Marko. It's doing just fine without us.'

'I can't go to the police. I'd end up in jail.'

'You have to let him go,' she repeated.

'But he killed her.'

I felt her go suddenly still beside me, and heard her swallow. I turned and saw a tear on her cheek. A gust of wind spread it across her face and it was gone.

'Do you know what it was like at Matthew's funeral?' she said, and I wasn't sure if she was changing the topic. I wasn't sure of anything. 'Have you ever seen an eleven-year-old buried? They waited six days. Waited for me to be found, and I was so tired when I got there, it all felt so hurried. I was in shock for most of it and when I try to think of it now it's just a blur. There were so many funerals. Our undertaker was doing five that day, so every-thing had to be done to a schedule. When we came out of the church there was another group waiting to come in, trying not to look at us. And inside it was so packed, there were so many peo-ple there. I felt as if the air was crushing me. He was only eleven and there were so many people.

'At an eleven-year-old's funeral you can't just pretend you see, you can't find any sense in it. So you go up there one by one and you talk about the good times, even though the good times are all over. You say, "at least there was this, at least there is some-thing we can cling to". And do you know what they mostly re-membered about him?'

She looked straight at me, like she expected an answer, but I'd never even met him.

'The little things, shit that happens every day, that you don't even think about. Some time he made somebody laugh, or did

something kind that he didn't have to do. It's not so much is it? Not much to come to at the end of it all. But it's everything too. That's what I ended up thinking anyway, sitting there. Somehow we can still do good things and somehow that still matters.'

Then she stopped, like there was nothing else that needed saying. Like then I would have to understand. But it wasn't my brother. I wasn't there, same as she wasn't in the hospital. It wasn't so easy to see past the Doctor's face. I shook my head again and again, until it felt like things were coming loose inside.

'I can't Lisa. He wanted to kill me. He killed her. I'm not letting him go.'

'Then fuck you!' she hissed at me, and before I could say anything she was standing, then storming off down to his grave, second row, three in from the right hand side. I didn't move, just sat there and watched her sink down on the dirt and even in the wind I could hear her crying.

She stayed there ten minutes, maybe longer. I tried to think things while she was gone, I tried to feel things, I tried to understand. But my mind wouldn't switch on. I was blank, numb. I was useless. When she came back she didn't sit down. She stood in front of me, legs set wide like she was getting ready to take another blow.

'You're pissing me off Marko, because I know that I'm right and I can't find a way of saying it. I can't make you understand. Just listen to this okay? I don't know why he tried to kill us, or why he killed Ms Jenkins. I don't know about him at all. I just know it's happened. But that's finished. It's not about him any more. It has to stop somewhere. Can you just not think about him at all? Can *you think about you instead?*

'See, you're not like him. Not yet. But if you leave him there you're a killer too, maybe even worse than him. Forever. Look around you. That's what you've contributed. Another hole in the ground for a family to stand over, feeling useless. That's not right. That can never be right. You do that and you've walked away from the only things that can ever matter, and I don't think you can ever walk back. If you can't change your mind now then he's still winning, because it's still not over, and it won't be over until you're dead too. You'll be stuck on the outside and I don't care how right it feels right now, one day you'll get the way it is, the way I can see it now, and then Marko it's going to be too late. Oh shit, Marko, you have to get this. You just have to.'

She stopped and stared me down. Her eyes were thick with tears and understanding.

'So you want him to get away with it?' I asked.

'No, it's too late for him. I want you to get away with it.'

My head was full of noise, old thoughts rearranging themselves, looking for a place to settle. I looked at her, her prickly short hair, her determined face, harder than anybody I knew, harder even than Rebecca, and I started to get it. Late, but maybe not too late.

'So how do I do it?'

She didn't answer. She just threw herself at me and pinned me against the bank. She squeezed me tightly, almost as tightly and as desperately as I squeezed her.

Doctor Found

Doctor Chris Shaw, who has been missing for two days, was today found alive in the building site of Palmerston North's new surgical wing.

Carl Stopper, an electrician called in to check on faulty wiring, discovered the doctor tied and bound in a locked room. Police say his attackers, who stole money and may have been trying to get access to drugs, are both Caucasian men in their late twenties or early thirties. It is possible they were living rough in the site which closed after the bankruptcy of H.J. Pickard construction. The doctor was kept in the hospital overnight for observation and is expected to make a full recovery.